ANTIBODY:

Love and War, Book 3

———◆———

R. A. STEFFAN

Antibody: Love and War, Book 3

Copyright 2018 by R. A. Steffan

All rights reserved. Printed in the United States of America. No part of this book may be used or reproduced in any manner whatsoever without written permission except in the case of brief quotations embedded in critical articles or reviews.

This book is a work of fiction. Names, characters, businesses, organizations, places, events and incidents either are the product of the author's imagination or are used fictitiously. Any resemblance to actual persons, living or dead, events, or locales is entirely coincidental.

For information, contact the author at
http://www.rasteffan.com/contact/

Cover design by Deranged Doctor Design

First Edition: August 2018

INTRODUCTION

This book contains graphic violence and explicit sexual content. It is intended for a mature audience. While it is part of a series with an overarching plot, it can be read as a standalone with a happy ending for the two main characters, and a satisfying resolution of the storyline.

TABLE OF CONTENTS

One...1
Two..13
Three..24
Four...36
Five...47
Six..58
Seven..71
Eight..84
Nine...94
Ten...104
Eleven..114
Twelve..131
Thirteen..140
Fourteen..153
Fifteen...165
Sixteen...174
Seventeen...188
Eighteen..201
Nineteen..209
Twenty..219
Epilogue..235

ONE

"Ryder, I am experiencing a possible system malfunction," Pax said. "I need an objective observer to aid in assessment."

Pax had to stoop to look through the door of the converted attic bedroom in the old farmhouse. Inside, it was almost completely dark. Only his enhanced cyborg senses allowed him to make out movement in the bed. Ryder stirred from where she had obviously been asleep moments before, wrapped in her new lover's arms.

"Pax?" she murmured, her voice raspy from her prolonged expression of delayed grief the previous day. "Just a minute…"

Another figure rolled over and a bedside lamp flipped on, illuminating her bedmate's groggy features. Temple blinked a few times, clearly trying to engage his brain after the unexpected awakening. "Is this an 'all hands on deck' kind of problem or a 'don't worry, this will just take a few minutes' kind of problem?" the human asked.

"There is no immediate danger to the people in this house," Pax told him. "Ryder, I would not disturb you so soon after the memorial ceremony—"

She cut him off. "Don't, Pax." He snapped his mouth closed and averted his eyes politely as she grabbed a pair of trousers, pulling them on. "If there's a problem, I don't want anyone else here trying to play doctor for you. That's my job. And prophets know I don't want you attempting to self-diagnose, either. Come on. Let's go somewhere with better lighting."

"Want me to tag along, you two?" Temple asked around a yawn.

Ryder hesitated for a bare moment. "Yeah... if you don't mind."

"Course I don't," Temple said, and rummaged for a shirt.

In the part of his brain that wasn't preoccupied with the impossible distress call he'd received a few minutes ago, Pax was gratified to observe Ryder's small—and uncharacteristic—act of reaching out. For too long, she had rebuffed all attempts by her friends to breach the protective walls with which she surrounded herself. While the change had clearly been a painful one for her, Pax thought it would almost certainly be healthier for her psyche in the long run.

When the pair was ready, he switched on the LED nestled amongst the implants at his left temple, using it to light the way down the cramped staircase leading to the main floor. The house was quiet, its timbers creaking as the temperature outside cooled more quickly than the temperature inside. Ryder indicated that they should enter the kitchen, where she turned on the overhead light.

She looked pale, her features drawn with the combination of recent injury and long-denied grief. Nevertheless, her movements were brusque and commanding as she gestured them to the table that dominated the center of the room. He followed the pair's example and sat in one of the mismatched chairs, not because standing was a problem for him, but because he knew sitting would help put the others at ease. Temple, in particular, had seemed uncomfortable in his proximity since their somewhat unfortunate first meeting.

Self-indulgently, Pax spent a moment trying to recall what it had been like not to inspire terror in strangers by his very presence, and failed.

Ryder scrubbed a hand over her face, as if to rub away her exhaustion. "All right, Pax. Give me details. What are your symptoms?"

"I have experienced an occurrence which I know to be impossible," Pax explained. "Either the present incident is not real, or my memory of the past is not accurate."

Ryder mulled that over for a moment. Temple frowned.

"Can cyborgs experience hallucinations?" he asked, a bit warily.

The medic shrugged her uninjured shoulder. "Pax's brain is a tangle of organic synapses and nanobot-constructed tech," she said. "In some ways, it's a delicate system. It's certainly possible, but I suspect there are additional possibilities that may become apparent on further inspection. Now, what are the two contradictory facts?"

Pax cocked his head. "I received a unique internal distress call originating from one of my batch siblings twelve-point-three minutes ago. It lasted for thirty seconds and then discontinued."

Ryder nodded. "And what's the problem with that?"

"I watched my batch siblings march into the decommissioning chamber seven years, two months, and eleven days ago. I watched as unit D-8 was vaporized. Yet this was D-8's embedded distress beacon. Both things cannot be true."

Temple blinked. "They... made you watch your fellow cyborgs being *killed*?"

Ryder's mouth twisted in displeasure, and if Pax could have felt regret, he would have regretted bringing up a subject he knew she found upsetting.

"Cyborgs have a distinct sell-by date, generally speaking," she said, her unhappiness coming through in her tone.

Temple's brows drew together in confusion.

"Early experimentation revealed that after a certain period of time, cyborg brains become unpredictable," Pax explained, "and therefore either useless or dangerous to our military handlers."

Ryder grunted. "To get around the problem, the military started 'decommissioning' them well before their expected failure date."

The human went a bit gray beneath his dark skin. "And by 'decommissioning,' you mean...?"

"Vaporizing," Pax confirmed.

Temple stared at him for a beat, his head shaking minutely back and forth as he sought words. "How in the hell did our society end up here?" he asked eventually. "How did our world... *get* like this?"

"Incrementally, and through effective use of psychological conditioning and propaganda," Pax replied without hesitation. "The organic brain is easily shaped, given enough time and resources."

The human sitting across from him pinched the bridge of his nose as if trying to root out a headache. "Yeah," he said with a sigh. "Shit. Isn't that the truth? Okay, so—next question. And I apologize ahead of time for the bluntness. But, if the rest of your cyborg batch reached its sell-by date, and your handlers made you watch while they were vaped, then how are you still here?"

Pax affected a shrug. "My systems failed early. I regained free will, but I was cognizant of the realities of being a cyborg. I had no wish to face immediate termination, or to know that my system failure had condemned my batch-siblings to early termination as a precaution. So I hid it."

Ryder's face grew hard, and again, he would have felt regret. He'd never determined if her reaction to the next part of the story was because she was angry with him for his actions—well, more accurately, for his *inaction*—or because she was angry on his behalf. He had considered asking her to clarify on a few occasions, but it did not appear to be a subject she cared to discuss if it was at all avoidable.

"I often pondered ways to save myself and my siblings from being decommissioned," he said instead. "But they would not have understood my desire to continue on after being ordered into the vaporization chamber, and I did not wish to be parted from them."

Ryder shifted, and her voice was tight. "They were your family."

Again, it might have been accusation or commiseration. He did not ask.

"Yes," he agreed. "They were. For obvious reasons, we were not warned ahead of time when the decommissioning of our batch grew imminent. It was not considered relevant or necessary information for us to have. We were merely ordered to report to a particular place at a particular time, and told to proceed one at a time into a chamber."

Temple still looked ill. "And the rest of your... batch siblings? They just walked right in, without question?"

"Of course. They did not have the capacity to do otherwise," Pax said. "I positioned myself at the end of the line. Each time one of them entered, there was a long pause, and then a burst almost too brief to register as their distress beacon activated automatically, and was cut off. I did not decide on a course of action until the last member of our batch other than myself stepped into the chamber. His designation was D-8. I felt his beacon activate; I felt it terminate an instant later as his body disappeared into a cloud of particles behind the viewport."

"What did you do then?" Temple whispered.

"I killed the scientists and guards overseeing the vaporization process, destroyed the surveillance equipment, and escaped," Pax said simply. "There is a reason the military does not usually allow cyborgs to live long enough to go rogue." His eyes flicked back to Ryder. "But we should return to the matter at hand. I would like you to run diagnostics."

Ryder raised a pointed brow. "I've been doing that for the last five minutes. Your systems seem fine from here."

Pax tilted his head to regard her. "I had assumed the diagnostics would be somewhat more in-depth."

She blew out a breath. "Fine. Here's a logic test for you. The following statement is accurate: I am lying to you. What's your response to that?"

Pax blinked at her. "Your declaration that 'the following statement is accurate' is inaccurate."

Temple's eyes moved back and forth between the two of them like someone watching a hoverball match. "Okay, time out. Are you two for real right now?" he asked.

Ryder threw up her hands. "Pax, I don't know what you expect from me. We're in a farmhouse in the middle of nowhere. The only technology I have access to is an antiquated comm system and a couple of fighters. I don't think either Hunter or Kade would be too impressed if I tried to convert their flight systems into a diagnostic lab for cyborg software."

"This is serious, Ryder," Pax said.

Temple braced an elbow on the table. "Okay, look. I'm running on, like, three cycles of sleep, and I can still think of two non-paradoxical possibilities for what you've experienced, right off the top of my head."

Pax moved his gaze to the human. "Such as?"

"One." Temple counted off on his fingers. "What you thought was a vaporization chamber was actually something else, and D-8 isn't dead. Two. Someone forged your friend's distress signal."

"Neither of those scenarios is at all likely."

"Are they any less likely than you having a malfunction that in no way affects your ability to think or hold a reasonable conversation?" Temple pressed.

"Yes," Pax told him without hesitation. "As I said, cyborg brains have a history of failure. I am already more than seven years past the recommended lifespan for the technology."

Ryder still wore a sour expression. "Does the phrase, 'it's not a bug, it's a feature' mean anything to you? The Regime vapes cyborgs because they're afraid of exactly what happened with you—

the recovery of free will. I've told you before that there's no reason I can see why your systems won't continue to function indefinitely. For the most part, the technology inside you is highly effective at maintaining physiological equilibrium. The only exception is that the organic brain is an amazing thing. Eventually, it finds a way around the programming and reasserts itself."

Pax stared right back at her. "Which implies that it might just as easily alter itself in a way that causes hallucinations or madness."

Temple shifted in his chair. "Ryder's right, though. We've been talking for some time now, and you don't sound mad. Or delusional."

"This method of diagnosis is inexact and unscientific," Pax complained.

"Welcome to the wonderful world of clinical psychology," Ryder said. "I took two classes in it about a dozen years ago, as I recall. I even passed both of them. Now, are you going to insist we wake the others to figure out what, if anything, to do about this distress signal? Or can it wait until morning?"

The knowledge that he had received a call for help from D-8 and he was doing nothing circled restlessly through Pax's synapses.

"I will wake the others," he said.

Not long after, all of the house's inhabitants, save its owners, were gathered in the homey kitchen, in varying states of wakefulness. It was unfortunate that Ash had already returned to the Capital, Pax mused, since his computer expertise might have been useful. The human had his own self-imposed mission, though, and it was not one that was helped by his occasional absences to assist the rest of them with whatever crisis loomed at the time. As he'd pointed out, he had already been gone for days, and the excuse of being ill would only be believable for so long.

So, Pax waited until Hunter, Skye, Kade, and Draven joined Ryder and Temple around the large table, and succinctly recounted what he'd already told the latter two. He left out, for now, his concerns about his systems status—tentatively willing to accept Ryder's assessment unless additional data presented itself.

Skye scrubbed her hands down the length of her face, pulling at the pale skin. "Good gods. Could we maybe have a couple of freaking days without some sort of new crisis? Is that really too much to ask?"

Of course, the current situation was not necessarily a crisis for anyone except D-8... if D-8 still existed in spite of Pax's belief to the contrary. The others mulled over Pax's report for a few more moments before speaking.

"It sounds like some kind of trap to me," Kade muttered. "Mysterious distress call from a dead cyborg, that only you can hear? *Please*. Do me a favor."

"That's a fair point," Hunter said. "To whom would such a distress beacon normally be directed?"

"To all the related batch siblings," Pax replied. "In cases of a joint military operation combining multiple cyborg batches, the connection could be altered to cross over to other groups. That seems unlikely to be a factor in this instance, however."

Hunter nodded. "And you are the only surviving member of your batch, correct?"

"Correct."

Kade grunted. "Right. *Trap.*"

"Are you compelled to answer such a distress beacon?" Hunter asked, watching Pax closely.

"In some instances," Pax said.

Ryder drew breath and spoke. "For most cyborg functions, there's a hierarchy governing response to stimuli. It wouldn't make sense to compel a cyborg to go to a batch-sibling's aid if doing so would compromise a mission directive deemed more important than the life of a single soldier." She waved a tired hand. "It's a programming thing. Ash could probably explain it better."

"No, that makes perfect sense," Hunter said.

"It does," said Draven. "Though it doesn't really answer if you feel compelled to respond here and now, in this particular circumstance, Pax. Do you?"

Pax considered the wording of his reply. "Compelled is not the correct word. However, I will respond, for reasons that include a need to determine if D-8 is still alive, and a need to investigate what might be new developments regarding the Regime's cyborg program."

"Am I talking to myself over here?" Kade asked. "*It's. A fucking. Trap.*"

"You are not talking to yourself," Pax assured him.

"Oh, good," Kade said. "That makes a change."

"But I must still investigate," Pax added.

Kade threw up his hands in evident disgust.

Hunter steepled his fingers. "Kade's point is a reasonable one, Pax. No one here is in a position to stop you, should you decide to take this action... though I would point out that doing so would require you to take either Kade's fighter or mine, which might leave the rest of us in a very tight spot should an emergency arise."

Pax weighed Hunter's words, aware that his assessment was accurate. Pax's batch sibling—if he still existed—needed his help. But his friends needed the fighters, and utilizing public transport was impractical for a cyborg. It seemed that this was to be the night for conflicting facts.

"I do not wish to place you in danger," he said. "Therefore it appears I will require alternatives. I have none at this point in time. Does anyone else?"

Kade looked like a man who sorely needed the abbreviated period of rest he was able to catch between bouts of neurotonin withdrawal, but he blinked bloodshot eyes and spoke. "Ryder, how about your new acquaintance? She seems like someone who might be interested in possible changes or problems with the cyborg program. Also, one with the clout to get the information she wants. Assuming you trust her that much?"

Pax lifted an eyebrow. It was an interesting suggestion, and one that had admittedly not occurred to him.

Ryder nodded. "She saved my life. I think she's trustworthy in any situation where our objectives align, certainly. Mind you, I've got no clue what her objectives actually *are*, but it's clear she's no friend of the Premiere, or the Regime."

Hunter looked approving. "Pax, is that acceptable to you? Assuming she agrees, will you allow

Ambassador Veila'ana a day or two to look into it before taking action yourself?"

It took Pax only a moment to consider it. If D-8 were alive and in imminent danger as the beacon implied, Pax could not get to him in time to make a difference—the coordinates of the distress signal originated from orbit on the far side of the planet. And if, as seemed likely, the situation was more complicated than simple physical peril during a battle, the mysterious ambassador was, in fact, in a better position to investigate. Even if every single line of Pax's programming was urging him to *act now*.

"Yes," he said. "That is acceptable."

"Very well," Hunter said. "You and Ryder decide how you want to word the message. Use the comm in Kade's fighter to send it, rather than our hosts' unit. Ash upgraded the encryption programs a few weeks ago, and it's the most secure communications channel we have access to at the moment."

Kade pushed to his feet. "I'll come with you and give you the new passwords. No point in me trying to go back to sleep now; I'll need an injection in a couple of cycles, anyway."

Ryder huffed out a breath and rose as well. "Come on, then. We might as well get this done. When she mentioned it to me, it sounded like Veila'ana only checked this communication line for messages once a day or so. No point in waiting."

Pax nodded and joined them, already focused on the best way to prioritize the necessary information.

TWO

If you'd asked young Nahleene Veila'ana what she wanted to be when she grew up, *spy* probably wouldn't have been her first answer. In fact, it wouldn't have been her second, third, or tenth answer, either. Dancer? Artist? Princess? Those would all have made the list. *Ambassador* would have gotten you a distasteful wrinkle of the nose. *Patriot*, a blank look.

All of which went to show how much things could change between the dreams of childhood and the stark realities of adulthood. Sitting at the private communications unit in the Vitharan ambassadorial residence, Nahleene kept a portion of her awareness directed outward, mentally mapping the area around her. As a telepath—thanks to her Maelfian mother—she was always aware of the hum of other minds nearby.

Even though she could only make direct use of her abilities while touching another person, the knowledge of other sentient beings' proximity was a useful one for an intelligence agent. These days, her life was a constant struggle to stay one step ahead of Ilarian surveillance, preferably without *looking* like she was staying one step ahead.

That was why she was currently composing and sending a standard report to the Vitharan government covering her experiences of the past few days, while fully aware that it was also being recorded for delivery straight to the intelligence forces of the Ilarian Regime. And even though the contents dealt with her embroilment in a prison riot and subsequent injury in the crossfire, she was perfectly fine with that.

Her report to Vithara had been carefully worded to avoid any information that would raise suspicions among her hosts in the Ilarian Capital. It was the other report she was preparing that her hosts would no doubt find problematic. That report, which was not bound for Vithara, would need to be sent in such a way as to avoid the government bugs riddling this grand old ambassadorial residence.

Nahleene was the offspring of a Vitharan father and a Maelfian mother, with all the complications and contradictions that came along with such a heritage. True, there was something to be said for knowing from birth onward how incredibly wanted you had been, since her existence rested on complex—and expensive—genetic manipulation performed in a lab dish.

It was extremely rare for species from different planets to be able to interbreed without assistance; Vitharans and Maelfians were no exception. Her parents had met, rather ironically, during her father's stint as the Vitharan ambassador to Maelfius. Theirs had been a grand love story, at least for the first couple of decades. After a few years, they'd been desperate enough for a biological child of their own that they were willing to spend a small fortune on the necessary genetic manipulation, and she was the result—one healthy female child, made to order.

Unfortunately, her parents' great love affair had eventually withered and died on the vine. Her mother went back to Maelfius, divorced in the eyes of Maelfian law and legally separated under Vitharan law, where divorce wasn't something that was really on the cultural radar.

Nahleene had been born on Vithara and been raised there for several years, but after her parents split up, she traveled back and forth between the two planets. Her citizenship remained Vitharan, but she'd grown to love her mother's peaceful and empathic people with a passion that persisted into adulthood.

Her physical appearance meant that she never really fit in among her mother's pale, sylphlike race, and the differences in her mental gifts also made her stand out as *other*. Because it had been assumed that her home would always be Vithara, her parents had insisted that her appearance favor her father's people. She was short and slender for a Vitharan, but not remarkably so. Her features tended a bit more toward delicacy, and her pale blonde hair—almost silver—was unusual enough that most people assumed it had come from a bottle.

All in all, though, anyone looking at her would think her to be a full-blooded Vitharan... albeit something of a scrawny one. Only a select few knew of her mental powers, and fewer yet of her sundry other physical differences.

She'd stumbled into her ambassadorial career for the same reason that many other children followed in their parents' footsteps—because she'd shown a knack for it after growing up around the diplomatic corps on two worlds, and because it made her father happy. She'd stumbled into her spying career for other reasons. Like almost all spies, she'd been recruited. Then, she'd discovered that it paid rather ridiculously well. And finally, what she'd learned about the Ilarian Regime so far scared the ever-loving shit out of her, making her realize how necessary her job as an intelligence agent was.

Rightly or wrongly, Vithara remained confident of its military superiority over its upstart descendants on the colony of Ilarius. There was a history between the two worlds, to put it mildly, but even more than a hundred and twenty years after the ancestors of the Ilarian Vithii fled the homeworld, Vitharans didn't consider the Ilarian Regime an actual *threat*. Not to them, anyway.

A threat to others? Sure. But the Vitharan philosophy of non-interventionism ran deep. All the Vitharan government was really worried about was keeping the trade routes open. The Vithii population on Ilarius was hungry for products from the homeworld, and Vithara was happy to provide those products for the right price. Beyond that, what happened on Ilarius was the Ilarians' business, as far as they were concerned.

To say that Nahleene disagreed with that assessment on a personal level was putting it mildly. But as a half-breed, she had a second home planet that was very much concerned about Ilarian business, and it was to that home she now turned her attention. Her report to her spymasters on Maelfius was stated in much different terms than the report to Vithara, and it would travel via a much more secure electronic route.

Maelfius was not a military power in the Seven Systems. They never had been, and given the empathy and delicacy of the people who lived there, they probably never would be. For that reason, they were rather uneasy whenever another planet in the local group showed signs of looking outward with an eye to conquest. It didn't take a huge stretch of the imagination to think that the Vithii Premiere might decide crushing the humans on Ilarius was no longer sufficient to feed his desire for power, and that other planets with limited military force were starting to look tempting.

The Premiere was little more than a fascist dictator at this point, and dictators always needed an enemy in order to hold onto power. Once the current enemy was crushed too badly to wave under the people's noses as a threat, it would be time to move on to a new enemy.

The Maelfian government wanted to be damned sure they didn't end up playing that role for the Regime. And Nahleene wanted to help them in that quest.

When she'd originally been approached by someone from Maelfian intelligence, she'd made it very clear that she wouldn't act in a way that harmed Vitharan interests. To her surprise, her contact had acceded readily to that demand. At first, she'd been given small assignments—things that would not raise too many eyebrows if they accidentally came to light.

As her superiors' trust in her grew and her own confidence in her abilities increased, her assignments became more in-depth. Not to mention more dangerous. When the alleged bioweapon attack on the humans in the Ilarian Capital occurred, things ratcheted up considerably. Since then, her orders from Maelfius were to find out what had really happened and determine what could be done to head off this apparent escalation in Regime aggression. Or, ideally, what could be done to unseat the Regime from power altogether.

In a case of highly unfortunate timing, she'd been off-planet when the bioweapon crisis hit—recalled to Vithara for a series of semiannual meetings. But she'd seen the leaked footage of the scientist's daughter, Skye Chantrell, delivering her impassioned plea to the human population of the Capital to drink the tap water containing an antidote introduced by a group of vigilantes. Nahleene had also seen clips of the rioting that had followed, and she'd jumped on a ship back to Ilarius that very day.

By the time she arrived, humans were dying, and conflicting reports of what had happened were flying left and right at light speed. Humans claimed that the Regime had released the bioweapon into the atmosphere over the Capital, and only the antidote introduced into the water supply days before had prevented genocide. The Premiere, on the other hand, claimed that a previously unknown insect-born disease had been detected in the Capital, and the government had undertaken immediate release of insecticide over the city to combat it.

Nahleene had a lovely piece of beachfront property in the Chichaar Desert to sell to anyone who actually believed the latter explanation.

Since then, she'd been poking her nose anywhere she could get it in hopes of gathering evidence against the Regime and—just as importantly—trying to figure out her next step. It wasn't immediately clear if Xandrie Kovak, the Premiere, was actively insane, or merely corrupt and power-hungry. One thing was certain—he was undeniably well-insulated, and Nahleene hadn't come anywhere close to him personally. She hadn't even come close to his inner circle, despite being the ambassador from Ilarius' foremost trading partner.

Every person on the planet was familiar with the distinctive figure from newsvids, and could recognize the spiky blue-dyed hair, hard eyes, and crisp military uniform at a glance. But as a real person—a living, breathing Vithii rather than a face for propaganda posters—Xandrie Kovak was a virtual ghost.

From what she'd learned since first coming to this planet a handful of years ago, anyone who could successfully assassinate him and turn him into an *actual* ghost would be doing the Seven Systems a huge favor. Frankly, after what she'd seen in the past few weeks, if the opportunity ever arose, she'd be fucking well tempted to do the honors herself.

She sighed and finished composing her report for Maelfian intelligence, concentrating on the first level of encryption. The rest of the security would be electronic, but even in this day and age, the message itself was in code—a system of letter and number replacement Nahleene memorized and altered every two weeks. It was a laborious process, but once she was done, the report outlined the abuses she'd seen in the prison, and, more interestingly, her contact with one of the mysterious vigilante group who'd been behind the mission to introduce the bio-agent's antitoxin into the water supply.

Just as she was completing the transfer of the message from her secure personal tablet to a coded side channel on the questionably secure comm unit, she felt the approach of a familiar, but not particularly welcome, presence.

There was no time to finish the transmission and close down the terminal. Also, the blasted thing had a bad habit of hanging when you tried to abort a transmission and shut it down before it was completed. With nothing else for it, she abandoned the unit in favor of returning to her desk, seating herself casually just as her government-provided butler entered without knocking.

She looked up from a random pile of papers, feigning boredom. "Yes, Lendel? What can I do for you?"

Lendel was an aged Vithii man with hunched shoulders and a receding hairline. He was also undoubtedly a Regime spy, who'd been foisted on her so his handlers in the government would have a pair of eyes on her at almost all times. Still... in the man's defense, he did make a mean pot of *charlat* stew and he could iron shirts like a champion. So there was that.

His narrow eyes made a quick scan of the room before resting on her.

"Forgive the interruption, Ambassador," he began in his reedy voice. "I wanted to confirm that you were still expecting the central district representative and his bondmate for dinner later this evening. If so, would you prefer to have the meal in the large dining room or the small dining room?"

"The small dining room is fine," she said, unruffled. "I'm expecting them at twenty-one hundred, and I believe their daughter will be accompanying them as well."

Lendel nodded, a single, precise dip of the head. "Very well. I will arrange for the meal to be waiting."

His eyes strayed to the comm unit, the glow from its screen showing that it was still powered up. Nahleene did not allow herself to react beyond following his gaze. His head tilted, and he crossed the room to the compact wall unit.

"You've left the comm unit on," he said mildly. "That's a security risk, Ambassador. Allow me to turn it off for you."

Nahleene made a split-second calculation of how long the transmission to Maelfius would have taken to complete. She could cross the room and touch him—exert her mental influence to confuse him or give him a dizzy spell—but Lendel was an old campaigner. Playing that card more than once or twice might clue him into the fact that he was being influenced somehow. That Nahleene was more than she seemed.

Banking on the fact that the transmission should be complete by now, and knowing that the backchannel method she'd used to send it would not leave any incriminating status messages, she decided to play it cool.

"Ugh," she groaned, as if irritated with herself. "Thanks. That's what I get for trying to multi-task at the end of a long day. I just sent my weekly report off to the home office on Vithara a few minutes ago, and I was trying to get some of this paperwork finished while it sent. I'm afraid I forgot all about it."

Lendel's polite smile did not reach his eyes. "It happens to the best of us, I'm sure. I'll just leave you to your work. Shall I ring you a half-cycle before your guests are due?"

She waved a careless hand. "Yes, you'd probably better. It's clear that my mind has more holes in it than a sieve tonight. Thank you, Lendel."

"Of course, Ambassador."

Nahleene went back to ruffling through her random papers, paying the old Vithii no outward attention, even as her mind tracked his progress into the depths of the sprawling house. The constant game of secrecy and avoidance between them was exhausting, but it would have made her hosts far more wary of her if she had objected outright to his presence.

Once she was certain he was occupied in the kitchen, she turned her attention to her final clandestine activity of the day. While she used the comm unit provided by her hosts to send outbound encrypted messages, her Maelfian contacts did not use it to send messages in to her. Instead, she had a complicated series of intermediaries set up, utilizing a private comm number, the communiqués from which were transcribed, coded, re-routed, resent, re-coded, and eventually ended up as computerized voice messages on her private tablet—a device that never left her person, and would therefore be almost impossible for her hosts to bug.

Humming to herself, she plugged in a pair of old-fashioned earbuds and called up the message program, swaying in place as though listening to music while she returned to her papers. There was only one communication waiting for her, but a small thread of surprise wove through her as she listened to it. The pen she was ostentatiously twirling through her fingers stilled as Ryder, her intriguing acquaintance from the prison riot, outlined a terse message, the words delivered in a computer-generated monotone.

Nahleene's brows drew together, new concerns and questions crowding in to join the existing ones. She took a deep breath and called up her schedule for the next few days, looking for a time when she could get away from her closely watched home and office for a few cycles.

THREE

"Any further contact from your batch sibling?" Kade asked, as he eased the two-seat fighter down through the hatch leading into the echoing hangar.

Pax shook his head, doing a final sensor check to confirm that no other craft had followed them during their final approach to the Capital. "No. Nothing since the initial data burst."

Kade maneuvered the compact ship into its berth and started powering down the engines. He'd agreed to accompany Pax to his meeting with Ryder's mysterious ambassador partly because his business and underworld connections in the Capital might come in handy, and partly, Pax suspected, because he was slowly going insane in the peaceful environs of his old friends' rural farmhouse on the southern continent.

Not only would the trip give Kade a chance to check on some of his business interests that were difficult to oversee remotely; it also allowed him to replenish his stash of neurotonin stabilizers.

Always assuming the two of them didn't end up in the middle of an ambush when they went to meet with Ambassador Veila'ana, of course.

Pax was still of two minds about the merits of their current plan, but at least his options were more numerous now that he was back in the city. If the ambassador proved either uninterested in their information or actively hostile, he could acquire a ship of his own here without too much trouble. He could also pay a visit to Ash, whose computer skills and access to tech might be useful for a more in-depth systems diagnosis than Ryder had been able to manage.

He'd left a brief message outlining recent events and warning their human ally of his and Kade's return to the city, but they hadn't yet heard back—not an unexpected development, given that Ash had been absent from his own ongoing business for several days recently. No doubt he was also busy dealing with damage control on his self-imposed mission to infiltrate the household of the Adjunct to the Clandestine Operations Office.

The last of the ship's systems powered down with a smooth hum, and Kade gave a grunt of satisfaction. This was one of his company's hangars, which meant their security concerns were minimal—for the ship, at least. Once they left, their *personal* security concerns would be somewhat greater than minimal.

However, there was one positive thing about the growing chaos in the Capital. It made the Regime's job harder. Maintaining security in the city was increasingly a losing battle, despite the government's attempts at cracking down on the populace.

Pax followed Kade down the ladder leading from the hatch. The other man stretched his back, spine popping, and sighed. A human woman wearing the uniform of the hangar employees and carrying a data padd crossed to them. Pax twitched the hood of his jacket forward, throwing his face further into shadow.

She didn't pay him any real heed, though, merely jerking her chin up in a quick acknowledgement. "Hey, boss," she said to Kade. "We weren't expecting you. Grigor recognized your codes and paged me. Everything cool?"

"Some unexpected business came up," Kade said tersely.

The woman nodded, unconcerned. "No problem. You need the employees out of here for the night, or should we go about our routine as usual?"

"It's business as usual, Rita," Kade said. "Just pretend we aren't here. In fact, give us twenty minutes or so, and we won't be."

She shrugged. "Sure thing. I'll make sure your fighter is prepped and waiting for whenever you need it. Oh, and that guy from corporate was here a few days ago. He wants to go over the quarterly numbers on Hangar Eight when you have time."

"I'll contact him while I'm in town."

Rita nodded and tossed Kade an ironic little salute as they parted ways. Pax followed Kade silently toward the back offices, and waited while he fired off a handful of quick messages from the communications unit on the desk. There was a row of lockers in the hallway outside. Kade opened one with a thumbprint scan and rummaged, emerging with a hanger of clothing suitable for a business meeting... or an upscale club.

He eyed Pax's dark trousers, military-style boots, and black, hooded trench coat. "How are we playing this?" he asked.

Pax shrugged. "Businessman and bodyguard."

"Whatever works," Kade agreed. He reentered the office and dressed quickly, exchanging his well-worn flightsuit and leather jacket for a tailored suit in charcoal gray that matched his eyes.

The clothing could not disguise the hard, almost gaunt cast of Kade's features, but it transformed his appearance to the casual observer. Among the Vithii members of their cohort, Kade and Ryder were the only ones who could don the disguise of respectability with any real conviction. Though it was quite possible that Ryder had gained too much notoriety after the prison riot to do so with any degree of safety now.

Hunter's tattoos were too recognizable, and hiding Pax's own cyborg facial implants would take a serious effort with professional-grade prosthetic makeup. Draven still carried the valuable asset of anonymity within his arsenal, but he'd grown up a lower-class criminal, and casting him as respectable was a stretch.

It was yet another way in which their strategic options were slowly but inexorably shrinking. Regardless of how helpful she might be in the current situation with D-8, gaining the assistance of the Vitharan ambassador was an important step forward for them. Of course, their meeting with her tonight also risked backfiring spectacularly if it turned out to be some sort of trap. If Kade was compromised, that risked both their last link to respectable Ilarian society and their financial solvency, since he ran the business interests that funded their needs.

Though Pax took no pleasure from gambling, his cybernetic upgrades meant he was quite good at it. This particular bet hovered right on the cusp of what was reasonable or worthwhile. He was also very cognizant of the fact that it was his less-than-rational need to follow up on D-8's distress call that had brought it about in the first place.

Kade ran fingers through his dark spikes of hair until they were no longer mussed, and shot Pax a sideways glance. "A place like this will almost certainly scan for weapons."

"Weapons are unnecessary," Pax assured him. To be any sort of threat to a cyborg, their opponents would have to be well armed, and if they were, he could simply take what weapons he needed from them. He did a quick mental calculation of the time, and reached inside an inner pocket. "It has been four-point-five cycles since your last injection. Take this before we leave."

He pulled out one of the hypo-injectors he was holding and passed it over, ignoring the way Kade's jaw tensed.

"Yeah. Okay," said his companion, and disappeared into the employee lav to dose himself with the drug that would keep his neurotransmitters stable for another few cycles.

That Kade now allowed select members of their cadre to personally hold doses for him was progress, of a sort. He considered Hunter, Draven, and Pax safe options when there was a risk he might be away from the secure time-released container on his ship for more than six cycles. Still, Kade feared that he might lose control of himself during an episode of withdrawal. For that reason, he refused to allow Ryder or any of the humans to carry it, in case he was able to overpower them, injuring them in his irrational desperation to overdose.

Having seen Kade in the throes of withdrawal, Pax considered that scenario unlikely to be an issue with any of them except, perhaps, Skye, who was not skilled at hand-to-hand fighting. However, he supposed it said something about Kade that he worried about such things. The man in question emerged from the lav a few moments later, looking pale and grim.

"Let's go," he growled. "The meeting is in less than a cycle."

Pax was well aware of that, but he did not comment. He only fell in behind Kade, playing the role of silent bodyguard, his face hidden in the depths of his hood.

Club Aurora was located near the government district, about half a cycle's walk from the hangar. Security in this part of the city was still fairly tight, but in contrast to the times when they were traveling with the more blatantly wanted members of their group, like Hunter and Skye, Kade took no particular technological countermeasures against the surveillance cameras dotting the streets.

They were only stopped once, and he coolly removed his fake identichip for scanning, gesturing for Pax to do the same. As ever, the appearance of confident respectability carried nearly the same weight as actual respectability, and no one questioned the presence of a hulking guard protecting a rich businessman in the restive atmosphere of the city.

The building housing the club where they were to meet with the ambassador utilized the same white marble neoclassical human construction as most of the government district. The whole area was a silent reminder of the way in which Vithii had taken over the colony. Ilarius had originally been settled by humans during the Great Diaspora, after their home planet of Earth became uninhabitable—one of many such colonies within the local star cluster.

It was already established—small, but growing—when a group of Vitharan resettlement ships arrived one hundred twenty-three years ago, seeking asylum after a civil war on their homeworld. The humans had a workable infrastructure on Ilarius, but the Vithii refugees had more advanced technology. Treaties had been struck, and for the most part, the colony world flourished over the following century.

But everything came and went in cycles, and eventually a Vithii nationalist movement with a charismatic leader gained enough traction that it led to their current circumstances. Pax wasn't certain why the Vithii zealots couldn't see that it wasn't just the human population of Ilarius that was going down in flames; it was the whole colony.

The susceptibility of meatbag brains to outside influence could hardly be overestimated, he supposed. Though, to be fair, hadn't it been Pax's own concerns about his rationality after receiving D-8's distress call that brought him here tonight? Perhaps he no longer had room to talk.

His musings were interrupted by their arrival at the door to the club. A well-dressed but un-amused bouncer guarded the entrance.

"Guests of Ambassador Veila'ana," Kade said unconcernedly. "Has she arrived yet?"

The bouncer consulted a data padd. "She's here. Identification?"

Kade handed over his chip, and Pax followed suit. The bouncer entered their information on his padd, which was unfortunate, though expected. Now they'd be forced to ditch these IDs for new ones, to prevent the possibility of their activities after meeting with Veila'ana being traced. Forging new identichips was both a time consuming business, and an expensive one.

Once they'd both been scanned into the system, the bouncer gestured them inside with a jerk of his chin. Kade strolled past as though he owned the place, Pax keeping pace a couple of steps behind his left shoulder. He glanced around, taking in their surroundings from both a tactical and an aesthetic perspective.

"Not one of Jago's clubs, I gather," he observed in a low voice.

Kade snorted. "Hardly. I doubt even he could afford the rent on this place."

It had been many years since Pax had cause to be in a place like this—elegant, tastefully decorated, filled with the elite and those who hoped to cozy up to them. Not since his days in the military, before his cyborg enhancement, in fact... and then, only on a handful of occasions. The rank of full Commander hovered on the edge of power. It was worthy of respect, certainly, but frequently overshadowed by the higher brass, who always seemed to be jockeying for political position.

No one had ever accused Pax of being a politician, and they certainly weren't going to start leveling such an accusation tonight. It was a good thing he had Kade along to fill that role.

As they entered the main part of the club, a quick scan identified the expected surveillance concessions—cameras, bouncers, and a handful of individuals dressed casually as attendees, but whose deliberate pattern of travel through the crowd marked them as either government snoops or plainclothes house security.

Kade was also running his eyes over the room, but with the casually interested gaze of someone looking for acquaintances and scoping out the bar. Pax identified the head of unusual platinum hair that marked their target before he did.

"Corner bar, third seat from the end," he murmured, for Kade's ears alone.

Kade nodded, and they made their way to the bar by a somewhat meandering route. Pax studied the ambassador with the part of his awareness that wasn't constantly scanning for threats. She was much as Ryder had described her— petite for a Vitharan, with her finely drawn features visible in profile. The sweep of her eyebrow was the same shocking silver-blonde shade as her hair, and an ebony hoop hung from her earlobe. She was dressed to impress, in a black slip of a dress that hugged her curves, displaying the sleek muscles of a runner or a swimmer.

The heavy earring swung as she looked up at Kade, who came to a halt by the empty stool next to her and caught the bartender's attention with a look.

"Whiskey, neat, and another of whatever the lady is having, on me," he said, his gravelly voice gruff.

Fortunately, their cover story did not require Kade to play at a seduction. Because if it had, Pax might have insisted they stuff Draven into a business suit instead, and take their chances. Veila'ana raised a pale brow, clearly amused, and accepted the drink when the bartender pushed it across to her.

"Ambassador," Kade said. "I hope we didn't keep you waiting."

She smiled, and laid a hand briefly over the back of Kade's. Pax saw the twitch of muscles as Kade controlled his instinct to jerk away from the light brush of a stranger's fingers.

"Not at all," she said. "I just arrived a few minutes ago myself. Come with me. I can hardly hear myself think out here. I've arranged for a private room in the back."

"Lead on," Kade said.

The ambassador rose from her seat and slid past, her fingertips grazing the back of Pax's hand as she did. She paused for a bare instant, her pale eyes flashing to his face, still cloaked in the shadow of the hood. The tiny hesitation was scarcely noticeable, however, and then she was leading them toward a hallway in the back, her hips swaying. Pax took note of the wickedly tall high-heeled shoes she wore, which made her relatively short stature less obvious to the casual observer.

Ryder would probably have some muttered comments to offer about practicality and the dangers of long-term joint damage, but there was no denying that the heels showed off the muscles of Veila'ana's calves to great advantage. Pax wondered if she often relied on her physical attractiveness to disarm the men around her.

She led them down the hallway, past a number of closed doors marked for employees, to one with a coded keypad over the handle. He took note of the code as her fingers flew over the buttons. A moment later, the lock clicked open. The room beyond was dimly lit, but clear of obvious threats. It smelled faintly of alcohol, Vithii body odor, and sex. Pax adjusted his opinion of the quality of the club downward.

Veila'ana entered, and they followed her. She closed the door behind them and re-engaged the lock. "Lights on full," she ordered, and the illumination rose, throwing the room into sharp relief.

Pax flickered an eyebrow upward when the ambassador pulled a small jamming device from her handbag and flipped it on. Kade looked positively amused, at least for him.

"Do I want to know how you got that jammer past security?" Kade asked.

"Hmm. They must have missed it somehow," Veila'ana said blandly. Her pale eyes moved to Pax, and her head tilted, assessing him. "Any other threats in here that you can detect? This should take care of the cameras and audio recording equipment."

"The room appears secure, otherwise," he replied without hesitation.

She nodded slowly. "You're the cyborg Ryder described in her message. The one who picked up the unusual distress beacon. I'm surprised you came in person."

With no reason to remain hidden, Pax slid his hood back and waited to see how she would react. She didn't, except to run her eyes over his features with a look of interest.

"No offense, but you seem remarkably unconcerned for someone locked in a room with a Vithii military cyborg," Kade observed. "It's not really the reaction he usually gets, to put it mildly."

Kade handed over his chip, and Pax followed suit. The bouncer entered their information on his padd, which was unfortunate, though expected. Now they'd be forced to ditch these IDs for new ones, to prevent the possibility of their activities after meeting with Veila'ana being traced. Forging new identichips was both a time consuming business, and an expensive one.

Once they'd both been scanned into the system, the bouncer gestured them inside with a jerk of his chin. Kade strolled past as though he owned the place, Pax keeping pace a couple of steps behind his left shoulder. He glanced around, taking in their surroundings from both a tactical and an aesthetic perspective.

"Not one of Jago's clubs, I gather," he observed in a low voice.

Kade snorted. "Hardly. I doubt even he could afford the rent on this place."

It had been many years since Pax had cause to be in a place like this—elegant, tastefully decorated, filled with the elite and those who hoped to cozy up to them. Not since his days in the military, before his cyborg enhancement, in fact... and then, only on a handful of occasions. The rank of full Commander hovered on the edge of power. It was worthy of respect, certainly, but frequently overshadowed by the higher brass, who always seemed to be jockeying for political position.

No one had ever accused Pax of being a politician, and they certainly weren't going to start leveling such an accusation tonight. It was a good thing he had Kade along to fill that role.

As they entered the main part of the club, a quick scan identified the expected surveillance concessions—cameras, bouncers, and a handful of individuals dressed casually as attendees, but whose deliberate pattern of travel through the crowd marked them as either government snoops or plainclothes house security.

Kade was also running his eyes over the room, but with the casually interested gaze of someone looking for acquaintances and scoping out the bar. Pax identified the head of unusual platinum hair that marked their target before he did.

"Corner bar, third seat from the end," he murmured, for Kade's ears alone.

Kade nodded, and they made their way to the bar by a somewhat meandering route. Pax studied the ambassador with the part of his awareness that wasn't constantly scanning for threats. She was much as Ryder had described her— petite for a Vitharan, with her finely drawn features visible in profile. The sweep of her eyebrow was the same shocking silver-blonde shade as her hair, and an ebony hoop hung from her earlobe. She was dressed to impress, in a black slip of a dress that hugged her curves, displaying the sleek muscles of a runner or a swimmer.

The heavy earring swung as she looked up at Kade, who came to a halt by the empty stool next to her and caught the bartender's attention with a look.

"Whiskey, neat, and another of whatever the lady is having, on me," he said, his gravelly voice gruff.

Fortunately, their cover story did not require Kade to play at a seduction. Because if it had, Pax might have insisted they stuff Draven into a business suit instead, and take their chances. Veila'ana

The ambassador did not move her attention from Pax, and he watched curiously as she approached him to stand a step away. Even with her high-heeled shoes, she had to crane upwards to meet his eyes.

"Most people are frightened?" she asked, still studying him.

Pax studied her in return. "The propaganda machine has done its job well. Though, to be fair, my enhancements do make me lethally dangerous to organics."

An odd smile twisted one corner of her mouth. "Not to all organics," she said, her tone dry.

She lifted a slender arm as though to touch her fingers to his face. Pax's hand shot out to intercept the movement without thought, but he was careful not to exert enough pressure to unintentionally damage her as he caught her wrist. The instant the bare skin of his hand touched hers, an explosion of... something... flooded Pax's synapses.

FOUR

Pax dropped the ambassador's arm and staggered back a few steps, landing in a heap on the carpeted floor, some distant corner of his memory identifying the sensation as mindless, staggering... *grief.*

"What the *fuck*?" Kade snarled, lunging to place himself between the slim woman and Pax's crumpled form. "Pax! *Report*! What's your status?"

Pax's status was... that he had no idea what his status was. He lifted one hand to his cheek, then pulled it away and stared at the clear, saline wetness coating his fingertips. His chest heaved, pulling air past the heavy weight pressing down on it like an echo of loss.

"He's all right," Veila'ana said. "Just give him a minute. The effect will fade quickly since it's not really his. Sorry, that was a bit more of an extreme reaction than I was expecting. I've never actually pushed emotion on a cyborg before."

Kade's voice was steel. "*You.* Stay right where you are. Pax—*talk to me, damn it.*"

Pax blinked, and blinked again, the sensation of crushing grief fading away like a mirage until nothing was left behind but the endless desert of logic. He rose slowly to his feet, staring at Veila'ana past the bulk of Kade's tense body.

"It appears the ambassador was able to telepathically press the emotion of grief into my mind," he said. "Which should not be possible with a cyborg."

"And now?" Kade pressed, all his attention still fixed on the woman standing in front of him.

"The sensation has passed. I detect no lingering effects," Pax reported, moving to stand at Kade's shoulder rather than half-hidden behind him. He frowned at the ambassador. "How?"

Kade made a low noise in his chest. "Forget how. Let's start with *why*? We're here in good faith for a meeting *you* requested, *Ambassador.*"

Veila'ana had the good grace to look sheepish, though she covered the expression quickly. "As I said, that was not the reaction I expected. However, you both need to know that despite appearances, I have the upper hand in this situation. I was intrigued to meet your friend Ryder last week, the unfortunate circumstances notwithstanding. But I have several questions relating to recent events in the Capital, and your part in them. Those questions need to be answered before I'm willing to risk myself on any mission relating to the Vithii cyborg program."

Pax was still processing the implications of what the ambassador had just done, which was impressive, to put it mildly. That being said, she was hardly in a position of power, locked in this room with them as she was. His initial scan of his surroundings had identified half a dozen items and fixtures heavy enough to be used as projectiles that could injure or kill a non-cyborg without getting in arm's reach. Pointing that out did not seem like something that would advance their objective, however.

"What are your questions?" he asked instead, ignoring Kade's low noise of irritation.

Veila'ana's eyes moved to Kade. "You are Ehkadian Finisterre, the son of two prominent Opposition members who were assassinated by agents of the Vithii First movement. You were a political prisoner for several years, and still suffer with neurotonin addiction after the guards' attempts to pacify you during that time. You head a modest business empire that straddles both legal and illegal concerns. And you are active in a small criminal group headed by a notorious fugitive—a group that also happens to be dedicated to fighting the Regime's attempts to crush the human population of Ilarius."

Kade swore under his breath, his muscles still coiled tightly.

"Did you get all that from touching my hand earlier, or is there a database somewhere that I need to pay someone to hack?" he ground out.

"No database," Veila'ana said. Her gaze pinned Pax, and he returned it with interest. "You are cyborg unit PX-12, and I could read nothing useful from you beyond your assessment of the events occurring at the moment I touched you. However, there *is* a government database of information regarding the cyborg program, one which I studied in some depth as soon as I received Ryder's message."

"A logical response," he allowed.

"You are the only known cyborg to have gone rogue without being subsequently captured and destroyed," she continued. "But, rather than embarking on an mindless killing spree, you have apparently allied yourself with a mixed group of

Vithii and humans for the purpose of meting out vigilante justice against your creators."

"These are statements. Not questions," Pax pointed out.

"Is your group the main resistance movement against the Regime?" she asked.

"What the hell kind of question is that?" Kade countered.

She crossed her arms. "Let's try it this way. What are your aims with regard to the current government?"

Pax cocked his head. "Since you have us at a considerable disadvantage, perhaps you could first tell us what *your* aims are with regard to the current government. Because, by all appearances, you are acting as an ambassador for Vithara while simultaneously spying on your host planet."

She appeared to consider her reply carefully. "My aims are to ensure that the interests of my government are protected at all costs."

Kade seized on this immediately. "Government? Or *governments*, plural? We all know Vithara doesn't give a flying fuck about Ilarius as long as the trade contracts keep coming. But I imagine Maelfius has other concerns about the Premiere and his growing lust for power."

The flicker in Veila'ana's expression combined with the slight elevation in her pulse told Pax that Kade had hit the target dead center. "Her heart rate just increased," he reported.

Veila'ana visibly weighed her options for several seconds before replying. "I represent interests that would prefer not to see the Premiere turn his attention outward to other member planets of the Seven Systems."

Kade nodded. "And would those interests consider the fall of the Regime to be a positive outcome?"

"That would depend entirely on what replaced it," Veila'ana said evenly.

"An interim government representing both human and Vithii citizens, geared toward a return to the previous tricameral representative system, but with new checks and balances in place to prevent a recurrence of the Premiere's rise?" Kade suggested.

Perhaps Pax should have expected that Kade, the businessman and obsessive organizer, had given more thought to the nebulous concept of *what came after* than the rest of them had done. It struck Pax how little thought *he* had devoted to the subject, and he realized that it was because he did not truly expect them to survive, much less succeed in their objective. He had been focused on the battle at hand, and given its likely outcome, he had lost sight of the larger war.

"I think I can safely say that the interests I represent would consider that a desirable outcome," the ambassador allowed.

Kade relaxed his tense stance marginally. "Then I believe our goals are in alignment. Unfortunately, the part you aren't going to want to hear is the part where we're a tiny group with limited resources. We're mostly playing defense against whatever the outrage of the day happens to be."

Veila'ana appeared to mull that over for a moment. "Maybe we can do something about that," she said. "If nothing else, the footage of the riots around the water treatment plant a few weeks ago shows that you're not completely on your own."

Kade acknowledged that with a short nod. "True."

Pax regarded the ambassador steadily. "Does all of this mean you are willing to investigate possible developments within the cyborg program?" he asked, knowing that the wider discussion was important, but still eager to get the meeting back on its original track.

"If you have reason to believe something's up, then I'm willing to look into it," Veila'ana said. "I would, however, like to have a better understanding of exactly what it is I'm supposed to be looking into."

"What information do you need?" Pax asked.

She raised a challenging brow. "All of it, for preference," she said. "We shouldn't linger back here much longer. It's too suspicious, even if no one can see or hear us directly."

It took him only a moment to decipher what she was suggesting. "You wish to take the information directly from my mind."

Kade shifted on his feet. "That didn't go so well the first time, Pax."

Pax looked at Veila'ana, gauging her reaction to his next words. "If you refer to the ambassador's actions when she touched me earlier, I believe that was intended as an attack rather than communication."

Her expression went still. "I prefer the word *demonstration* to the word *attack*. And it was not, as I said earlier, a demonstration I expected to yield the results it did. I'd only intended to make a point."

"As you say. However," Pax continued, "if Kade is referring to your attempt at the bar, it appears the first connection with my mind was not as fruitful as expected."

"Your mind is different from a non-enhanced Vithii," Veila'ana said. "But I think I have a better read on you now, and I'm confident that if you actively recall the relevant information, I'll be able to see it."

Kade looked between them, clearly unhappy. Although, for Kade, that might not be a relevant observation, since happiness was not a state Pax much associated with him.

"It's your call, Pax," he said, "but she's right that we need to move this along."

"I agree to the mental contact," Pax told her.

Kade exhaled audibly, and, as predicted, it was not a happy sound. He crossed to stand by a table next to the low sofa they'd all been ignoring. Pax noted the way he leaned with a hand near the base of the table lamp resting on it—one of the items Pax had catalogued as a potential throwing weapon earlier—and knew that as ever, Kade had his back despite his grumbling. At the first indication of a mental attack against him, that lamp would be sailing toward the ambassador's head within an instant.

Pax did not expect such an attack, however. It would not benefit Veila'ana in any way that he could see, and she seemed a practical person from their interactions so far.

Now, she approached him and gave him another assessing look. "I'm going to touch the side of your face. When I do, think of whatever information you believe may be relevant to the task at hand."

"I understand," he assured her, and stood motionless as she raised her fingertips to his right cheek and temple—the side of his face that was bare of implants.

As he had expected, there was no explosion of unfamiliar emotion this time. In fact, there was only the faint hint of warmth where her skin touched his. He took a moment to wonder when the last time someone had touched him in such a way might have been. A moment later, he became peripherally aware of a softer brush of sentiment. Not an attack, just... a hint of sadness not his own.

Again, it was suddenly difficult to focus on what he was supposed to be doing, rather than latching onto that long-forgotten sensation and trying to decipher how it was possible that he could even register it, so many years after his emotion centers had been ripped out and replaced with circuitry.

"Think of the distress beacon," the ambassador murmured.

Pax took her audible command to mean that she was unable to communicate specific messages telepathically, at least to a psi-null individual like him. He wrested his attention away from the subtly enticing brush of her emotions and organized his thoughts.

The mental contact turned out to be a surprisingly efficient method of delivering information. Pax recalled an overview of his recruitment into the program as a Vithii soldier. His enhancement, along with the nineteen other soldiers in his group—his batch siblings. The experience of undergoing partial systems failure and unexpectedly regaining his free will. Being scheduled for decommission and watching his batch siblings walk into the vaporization chamber. Hearing their distress beacons cut off one by one as they were destroyed. Being the last one left. Attacking the guards and escaping.

He did not linger on the events of the intervening seven years, instead jumping forward to three nights ago, when D-8's emergency beacon unexpectedly—and impossibly—activated inside his head. As his focus shifted away from organizing and recalling the relevant events, he once more became aware of the bittersweet swirl of emotion that was his only hint of the ambassador's telepathic communion with him.

Without meaning to, he tried to identify and sort through the tangle of feelings, drawing on half-forgotten experience from his life before the program. Sadness was still there, he decided. Also, anger. And... disgust?

Veila'ana's fingers slid away from his cheek, breaking the connection. Pax blinked, recalling himself to the outside world. The ambassador looked pale beneath her copper-colored complexion. Of course, he realized. She would, after that. She might not have evinced the same fear most people experienced in his presence, but after seeing firsthand what he was and what he had done, disgust was certainly a natural enough reaction.

The nerves along his cheek and temple tingled in the aftermath of her touch, and he rubbed absently at the skin.

"All right, Pax?" Kade asked gruffly.

"Yes," he replied.

"I'll look into this, as soon as I'm able to arrange a way to get access into the program," Veila'ana said, her expression giving away nothing. "In fact, I might have an idea about that already."

"The distress beacon included coordinates," Pax said. "I will give them to you. The location is in low planetary orbit on the far side of Ilarius."

She nodded thoughtfully. "That would make sense. According to the most recent information in the government database, the R&D portion of the program is located on an orbital platform as a security measure."

"If you think you can get in there somehow within the next few days," Kade said, "we'll hunker down here in the Capital and wait to hear from you. Is there a better way to reach you than the remote comm code?"

The ambassador's lips quirked downward. "Not a secure one, no. But I'll start checking the remote comm twice a day rather than once. Do you have access to the same communications device I contacted to arrange this meeting?"

"We do," Kade said. "I'll arrange to have it monitored by someone trustworthy at all times. Let us know when and if you're able to set something up."

"I will," she said, and took a deep breath, as though steeling herself. "All right. We need to get out of here before the wrong people start getting curious about what we're up to. You go first. I'll follow in a few minutes."

"Your assistance in this matter is appreciated, Ambassador Veila'ana," Pax said.

She lifted a pale eyebrow. "Don't thank me. I haven't done anything yet." Her eyes met his, and he thought he could detect traces of the emotions he'd felt from her when her mind touched his as she continued, "And seeing as how I've been poking around in your minds, you both might as well call me Nahleene. It seems silly to stand on ceremony at this point."

"We'll wait to hear from you," Kade said. "Try not to get killed. At the moment, you're just about our best bet for a meaningful ally."

The ambassador—Nahleene—snorted. "I'll keep it in mind. Now, get out of here, you two. I'll be in touch."

Pax flipped his hood up to hide his face and let Kade herd him out of the private meeting room. As the door shut behind them, he once more took up his position behind Kade's shoulder, becoming the anonymous bodyguard of an equally anonymous businessman. Kade didn't linger, but headed for the door and into the hazy night air beyond. When they reached a quiet stretch of roadway, he flicked his gray eyes back to meet Pax's.

"This vulnerability to telepathic contact," he said. "Is it going to pose a problem?"

Pax thought of the warmth of Nahleene's fingertips... the sense of genuine emotion washing across his synapses like rain over dusty crops. The sharp reaction as he catalogued her sense of disgust through the tentative connection.

"No," he said. "It will not be an issue."

FIVE

Later that night, Nahleene lay in bed, staring into the darkness above her. Thinking. Everyone in the Seven Systems knew about the existence of the Vithii military cyborgs on Ilarius. She'd been quite young when word of the program had first leaked, but she still remembered the resulting moral outcry.

She remembered her father shaking his head grimly, his square jaw set and his heavy brow furrowed in distaste. She remembered seeing newscasts of the system-wide protest marches on the holovid, along with pundits endlessly debating the question of whether such a thing could be ethical as long as the people undergoing the procedure gave informed consent beforehand. Much of it had gone over her head; but then, she'd still been a child.

The political outrage had simmered for a year or two, and then slowly died away as the public's fickle attention shifted to something else. The Ilarian government had been careful to keep most of the details under wraps during the following few years of research. A decade passed, and the whole thing was largely erased from the public consciousness except for the occasional article in the press or scientific journals.

At least, it was erased right up until the day the Ilarian military unleashed a small unit of cyborg shock troops to put down a civil uprising on a lunar facility. The facility acted as Ilarius' chief extraplanetary trade port, and the group of human and Vithii opposition activists who had taken control of it didn't stand a chance against the creatures sent to destroy them. Their gruesome deaths—in what was arguably a lawful offensive by the elected government to retake an important strategic asset from rebels—catapulted cyborgs back into the public eye.

From that day onward, they were established as an effective military weapon, terrifying not just for their ruthless efficiency in meting out death, but also because of what they *were*. Vithii, but not. People, but not. Sentient, but with no will beyond their orders to kill.

Not much later, the first reports emerged of cyborgs going rogue and attacking anyone unlucky enough to be within range. This was enough to inspire new levels of horror among the populace, but the incidents were quickly followed by reassurance from the government that the problem had been researched, understood, and dealt with. And, indeed, there were no new reports of rogue cyborgs in the years that followed.

Now, Nahleene knew why.

The military had *dealt with* the problem by vaporizing its cyborgs before their minds and software developed faults, keeping them for only a handful of years before putting them down like rabid animals and replacing their ranks with fresh converts. And it had worked, after a fashion—in every case, apparently, except for one.

She thought of the mind she had touched that evening, a mind unlike any other she'd ever had contact with over the course of her lifetime.

The cyborg's companion, the Vithii called Kade, was a bitter shell of a man. An individual of shocking intelligence and will, but driven almost solely by his desire to tear down the Regime that had already torn down his life. She'd felt his gut-deep loyalty to the small band of fighters trying to stand against the power that now ran his world, true, but she'd also seen how little he cared for his own life after all the things that had been done to him.

Pax, though.

She could not think of him as PX-12. As a *unit*. He was a walking, talking contradiction—a killing machine that had regained his sense of self and constructed a functioning moral framework from the wreckage of his former life. A being whose capacity for emotion had been burned out of him, but who nonetheless fought for freedom and claimed others as friends. A victim of technology who had somehow wrested that technology under his own control, and now used it for a noble purpose.

After seeing his past laid bare, she'd ached for him. Her feelings of anger and disgust over what had been done to him and his fellow cyborgs had nearly overwhelmed her. She'd known right then that she couldn't ignore the pair's request for her help.

It didn't matter whether Pax's mysterious distress beacon was a mistake, a malfunction, or a clue to some new and horrific plot. The cyborg program was a crime against sentient life, and it needed to be stopped. Though whether either one of Nahleene's government employers would agree about that point was admittedly something of an open question.

Okay... that's a lie, she admitted to herself. It wasn't an open question. She was either a diplomat or a spy, depending on whom you asked. Neither job entailed single-handedly closing down a controversial military program on her host world.

And right now, that was perfectly all right with her. First thing in the morning, she would renew her acquaintance with her old *friend*, the Under-Minister for Military Logistics. And she would convince him—with or without utilizing her mental abilities—that he wanted to show off the latest developments in cyborg technology to her.

Because, *hey*, maintaining relationships was a vital part of diplomacy, wasn't it? And learning about secret programs was a vital part of spying. Beyond that... well... she'd just have to wait and see.

Jodor Erisuel was a slimy bastard, and it hadn't taken a surreptitious peek into his thoughts for Nahleene to figure that out. In addition to being unpleasant company and corrupt to the core, the Under-Minister was also an attempted murderer. He'd tried to have his estranged bondmate killed in order to mitigate a legal scandal, and when that hadn't worked, he'd nearly performed the deed himself during the recent prison riot.

Nahleene had taken it upon herself to prevent that murder by touching Jodor's mind and pushing exhaustion on him before he could pull the trigger. He'd collapsed like a sack of grain immediately afterward.

Normally, something like that would make one's ongoing professional relationship with a colleague... *awkward*. In this case, however, Nahleene had possessed the presence of mind to push confusion on him at the same time.

She'd been injured, waking from unconsciousness to find him about to shoot Ryder. That had not been an acceptable outcome, so Nahleene took matters into her own hands and neutralized the threat. After Ryder and the human prisoner she'd been sent to retrieve escaped, Nahleene spun a tale for Jodor Erisuel that painted him as a hero. He'd awakened confused and groggy, at which point she told him how he'd saved her from a hostage situation by chasing off the two prisoners, though he was stunned unconscious in the struggle.

She knew he still had suspicions. But she also knew he needed the cover story she'd given him for political purposes. There was no indication that he'd guessed the truth about her telepathic abilities, and so they'd maintained a somewhat uneasy truce since then.

It was just her luck that the Under-Minister also happened to be a key to the back door leading into the place she needed to go. His department of Military Logistics did not encompass the research part of the cyborg program, admittedly, but it was still very much involved in the utilization of the end product. And Nahleene was willing to bet that professional courtesy meant if Jodor wanted a tour of the cyborg R&D lab, he could get it—hopefully, with a diplomatic guest in tow.

Hence, the rather stilted working lunch date through which she was currently suffering. She was honestly a bit surprised Jodor had agreed to it at all. It looked now like he was starting to wish he hadn't.

"The cyborg program isn't part of my department," he told her, fiddling idly with the stem of his wine glass. "You'd need to talk to someone in weapons research."

"I understand that you don't have direct oversight, Under-Minister," she said. "But your departments do overlap in some ways. I was merely hoping you might be able to speak to someone who could arrange it."

His eyes narrowed, and she was struck—not for the first time—by how unappealing he was to her, despite his rugged Vithii good looks. *Politicians—ugh. Can't stand 'em*, she thought sourly, aware that there was a degree of hypocrisy involved in a spy belittling someone else for being inauthentic. Still, at least *she* was being inauthentic in pursuit of a higher cause—not for self-aggrandizement.

"I can't help noticing that your interests are rather... eclectic, Ambassador," he was saying. "First prison conditions, and now cyborg research—?"

She made her eyes wide and innocent. "As a diplomat, it's my job to familiarize myself with my host planet. I must say, Ilarius' government fascinates me."

And repels me, she didn't add.

Fluttering her lashes at him clearly wasn't working. His mouth twisted down as he replied, "The cyborg program is sensitive. Our enemies would just love to get a peek inside at some of the work researchers are doing right now. We don't exactly give guided tours."

How interesting. So the researchers were hard at work on something new, were they? Nahleene tallied one point into Pax's column. It looked like it was time to break out the secret weapon.

She let her hand slide across until her fingers covered Jodor's. He stared down at the offending appendage as though she'd just done something distasteful, but she was already pushing eagerness to please through the delicate connection.

It was something of a pity that he didn't find her sexually attractive, she supposed, but she couldn't bring herself to be truly unhappy about it. The idea of him simpering at her was positively repulsive, given what she knew of his background with his bondmate.

Besides, her hybrid genetics made sexual interaction with Vithii males iffy. Her mother had insisted on some alterations to the Vitharan genome related to her mating gland and pheromone production. So, while she could pass visually, her body didn't always produce exactly the right scent markers during physical interplay.

For this reason, it was generally safer for her to stick to non-sexual methods of persuasion. Jodor blinked rapidly, still staring down at her hand on his, but with the expression of someone who'd lost his train of thought and was struggling to regain it.

Right… let me just help you out with that, asshole.

"So you're willing to set up a tour of the orbital platform where this R&D work is going on?" she asked. "Oh, that's *brilliant*, Under-Minister. I'll make certain to include your name in my next report to

Vithara. They'll be *terribly* appreciative of your support and assistance."

He opened his mouth and closed it, still with that *'brain rebooting, please stand by'* expression on his face. When he finally spoke, his tone was unsure. "I... don't think..."

"That it will be a problem?" she finished for him, pressing harder against his mind. "That's wonderful. I'm hoping to schedule this in the next few days—I'm sure you understand how it is."

Again, his lips moved for a few seconds before anything emerged. "Yes... I'd like to try to accommodate you... Ambassador..." He shook himself as if trying to refocus, and she let her hand slip away from his. "I'll just... uh... need to speak to the Minister for Weapons Research and arrange it. I know how important this tour is to... relations with Vithara."

"That's right," Nahleene said earnestly. "I feel this could be a huge turning point in both our careers."

He nodded a bit uncertainly, though his expression was clearing now. "Yes. Quite so. I'll do my best to organize things and contact you with the itinerary in the next day or two."

"Wonderful. I knew I could count on you," Nahleene said cheerfully, returning her attention to the food on her plate.

Four days later, Pax sat in the co-pilot's seat of Kade's fighter, hidden behind one of the orbital solar arrays that generated remote power for many of Ilarius' off-planet bases and outposts. The array played havoc with scans in the immediate area, which made it quite useful when one needed to stay undetected while in low orbit. Of course, that also meant the fighter's systems were a mess as long as they were close to the thing.

"I'd feel better about this whole plan if Ash was answering his fucking comms," Kade muttered. "The complete lack of backup on this mission is asking for trouble."

"His lack of immediate response is not unexpected," Pax said, not for the first time in the past few days. "He was absent from the Capital for some time after the prison riot. And he had no reason to think that we would be leaving the safehouse on the southern continent. No doubt he is currently... detained."

His companion made a noise of distaste, low in his throat. "No doubt he is... the crazy bastard."

"Were you able to contact Hunter with an update?" Pax asked.

"I sent an encrypted data packet to his fighter's comm unit last night and received an automatic confirmation of receipt," Kade said. "If he's trying to send a reply now, we won't get it. Not while we're cozied up to this blasted thing." He gestured at the solar array visible through the clearsteel cockpit dome.

It was true. The array was situated practically on the doorstep of the orbital platform from which D-8's distress beacon had originated, but it was still taking nearly all of the fighter's power to keep an eavesdropping channel open for communications originating from those coordinates. The possibility of picking up anything from the southern continent through the interference was nil.

Kade's assessment about backup was not completely accurate, however. He and Kade *were* the backup—specifically, they were Ambassador Veila'ana's backup. Even now, she was approaching the orbital platform that housed the cyborg research program, a passenger on the ship belonging to Jodor Erisuel, of all people. Pax had filed that bit of information away for future consideration, since he had additional business to conduct with the Under-Minister for Military Logistics if the opportunity presented itself.

How that business would mesh with the current mission remained to be seen. As it stood now, their plan was nebulous and would no doubt evolve on a minute-by-minute basis. He and Kade were here to monitor the orbital platform's communications while Veila'ana was aboard, in case something went wrong.

The amount of security around the cyborg project meant that the ambassador had no way to contact them directly. She had arrived at the platform as a passenger on the Under-Minister's orbital transport, and would leave the same way. They would only learn of what was happening if it was deemed important enough to merit a comm burst from the platform to the Capital. And if that happened, it would be a sure sign that things had gone badly for her.

A beep and a hiss informed Pax that the time-release storage safe where Kade kept his stash of neurotonin had just released another dose. Pax hadn't noticed any obvious onset of withdrawal symptoms yet, but the way Kade grabbed for the hypo-injector made it apparent that he was already feeling the cravings.

Kade's shoulders were stiff as he turned half away in his seat and injected it with a hand that shook perceptibly. As if *Pax* would have any sort of reaction or opinion regarding his need for a fix. The only thing Pax cared about was that the timing was reasonably good. It was unlikely Kade would need another injection before Veila'ana completed her tour and departed for the Capital again, which was strategically helpful in the event that they needed to act quickly.

The comm channel crackled to life. A static-riddled message acknowledging successful docking procedure with the Under-Minister's ship emerged from the speakers, barely intelligible.

"Can we clear that shit up any better than this?" Kade asked, tossing the spent injector into the cockpit's waste receptacle. "We'll be lucky if we can hear a damned thing.

Pax said nothing, but called up the comm system interface and started fine-tuning it further. If things went wrong on the station, they'd need to move fast or risk losing one of the few influential allies they had.

SIX

The moment Nahleene stepped off the Under-Minister's transport, she knew something was wrong. She had expected to sense the minds of the Vithii scientists, guards, and staff on the orbital platform. She had not expected them to be the *only* minds she sensed.

Her meeting with Pax had demonstrated that the feel of a cyborg mind was noticeably different than the feel of an unconverted mind. Ripping out a being's emotional centers had consequences, and while she could not sense the artificial circuitry added to a cyborg brain, she could most definitely sense the truncated organic remains of the original person.

There were no minds like that here.

Covering her unease, she allowed Jodor to herd her through the airlock and into the station. There, they were met by an official in military garb, flanked by two armed guards. The official had the bearing of someone who thought there were far better things he could be doing than giving a guided tour to a couple of ground-side paper pushers. Nahleene only hoped that as paper pushers went, Jodor had enough clout to ensure that their hosts followed through on whatever arrangements he'd made with them.

She also hoped Jodor didn't decide to snap out of his mild daze while they were under the military official's watchful eye. She'd already had to reinforce her mental influence over him once on the trip here, when he'd frowned at the transport's controls as though suddenly unsure what he was doing. He'd looked up at her in confusion, his mouth falling open to say something, but she'd cut him off with a brush of fingertips over his cheek.

For some reason, the fact that he was a reasonably strong-willed person irritated her. Someone so slimy should also be a coward. A loser. He didn't deserve to have redeeming characteristics. Regardless, she'd hit him with another strong push, silently reminding him that he really, really wanted to impress her. She'd put everything she had into channeling the feeling that making her happy would make other good things happen, and a moment later he'd blinked, refocusing on the controls.

So far, it was holding.

In fact, it appeared that having an audience in the form of the station personnel made Jodor determined to flaunt his influence. So much the better.

"Captain Tarell," he was saying, "it's good to see you again. I can tell you're busy, so I won't keep you long. Is the layout still the same since my last visit?"

Captain Tarell looked no more impressed by Jodor's posturing than Nahleene felt. To his credit, none of his disdain came through in his tone as he said, "Broadly, Under-Minister. We have recently expanded the micro-surgical suites into a fourth bay."

"Good," Jodor said. "I'll handle the tour myself, in that case. No need for you to take time away from the important things you must have scheduled."

The Captain still appeared disapproving. Not for the first time, Nahleene wished her abilities were more useful at a distance. She might be able to sense the presence of other minds around her and get a good idea of whether they were Vithii, Maelfian, human, or cyborg—but without touching the captain's skin, she had no idea whether Tarell was more likely to order mugs of hot *edelveen* for them, or pull out a sidearm and escort them to the brig.

He did neither. "Very well," he said, with a hint of steel in his voice. "These guards will accompany you. If you need assistance, just ask."

Nahleene could live with that. It would have been too much to hope that the station captain would let them wander around a top-secret project completely unaccompanied. Jodor apparently agreed, since he only said, "As you wish, Captain," and gestured imperiously to the guards to follow. They did so without a word.

Jodor led them down a central corridor toward what Nahleene expected would be the hub of the platform. Most orbital stations were built along roughly the same lines, since space was at a premium on anything constructed outside of a planet's atmosphere. Her assumption was proven correct when they entered an open area with corridors leading off in every direction like spokes. At the end of each spoke, there would be a cylindrical section containing a workspace or lab—part of the outer wheel-shaped structure familiar to space-faring races across the galaxy.

The central hub appeared to be wholly administrative. Clearly, the scientific heavy lifting took place on the wheel. Oblivious to the fact that his commentary was unnecessary, Jodor pointed out the workstations and comm arrays as though they were something important. A few moments later, he came to a halt, looking around at the identical corridors branching off every which way. They were labeled, but only with seemingly random strings of numbers and letters.

"Guard," he said, "remind me which corridor leads to the original surgical suite."

"This way, sir," said the expressionless Vithii soldier behind Jodor's left shoulder, and indicated a corridor a few meters along.

"Ah, yes, I thought that was the one," Jodor said immediately, and Nahleene had to stop herself rolling her eyes.

At the end of the passageway, clearsteel doors led into the wheel, while lift doors stood open on their right. Jodor entered the lift, waited for the rest of them to follow, then punched the button to take them up one level. The lift opened onto an observation room with an unobstructed view of the medical bay below.

Nahleene walked forward, drawn by curiosity and no small degree of trepidation. A full medical team occupied the room, most of them clustered around a prone figure on the operating table. The male Vithii was huge, naked, and pale as wax. Electrodes dotted the parts of his body that weren't sliced open and being implanted with things Nahleene didn't have a name for. Her stomach rolled, and she pushed the reaction down, having no time for it.

"Ah, we're in luck," said Jodor. "I was hoping they'd have one on the slab for us."

Nahleene couldn't take her eyes from the flat green lines playing across the monitoring equipment. "Tell me what's happening," she said, not wanting to make assumptions without the facts.

"This is the latest breakthrough," Jodor boasted. "The answer to many of the problems that have plagued the cyborg program since its inception. Until recently, in order to make a cyborg, the military had to sacrifice an organic soldier. The project took the strongest and the best, and made them better. But it also made them different. Many of the candidates might otherwise have gone on to rise through the ranks, eventually becoming captains or admirals."

The strongest and the best. Nahleene thought of Pax, and didn't doubt it.

"By turning them into cyborgs," Jodor continued, "we were unintentionally weakening the future leadership of the Ilarian military. Not only that— we were also ensuring that those cyborgs would have to be decommissioned in only a few short years. It was a waste, all around."

Nahleene continued to stare at the Vithii on the table below them. No heartbeat. No brainwaves.

"And now?" she asked, her mouth growing dry.

"Our scientists have come up with the perfect solution," Jodor said proudly. "All of the problems with the software stemmed from its incompatibility with an organic brain. The remnants of the cyborg's mind tried to rewire its own neurons to compensate for the technology, like those rare medical cases you hear about where a person with brain damage to the language centers somehow learns to speak again."

He tapped his temple by way of demonstration. "When the equivalent of that happens to a cyborg, everything goes haywire. And the blasted things aren't much use if they don't follow orders and behave predictably."

"But your scientists have found a way around that?" she pressed, fairly sure she wasn't going to like what came next.

"They have." Jodor gestured at the scene playing out below them. "Cyborgs use bots to maintain their systems and repair any injuries to their organic components. A few months ago, someone realized that if you're going to put that much nanotech inside a Vithii body, there's no particular reason you need to start with a live subject."

Nahleene couldn't help the way her breath caught.

"You mean... they're using *dead* subjects?" she asked, just to be certain she hadn't misunderstood.

"Exactly." Jodor sounded smug.

Below them, the medical personnel were closing up the incisions in the male Vithii's face and chest. One of the doctors connected a syringe to a port in the metallic filigree of tech on the left side of the cadaver's chest, and emptied the contents into it.

"It looks like they've just introduced the active bots into the subject's bloodstream," Jodor said, pointing at the woman as she removed the syringe and dropped it in a sterile bowl held by another figure wearing a lab coat. "Next, they'll upload the AI into the cranial circuitry."

Nahleene tore her eyes away from the scene in the surgical bay below her to look at Jodor. "They're utilizing artificial intelligence?"

He blew out a snort of amusement. "Well, the downside of dead people is that they're not terribly high on the IQ scale. In the past, the cranial upgrades were used to provide additional computing power and to interface with outside systems. But they were still controlled by the soldier's organic brain—just with the emotions and free will removed."

As if that wasn't bad enough, Nahleene thought, feeling ill again.

"The research teams are always thinking ahead, though," Jodor continued, oblivious. "They've been downloading the minds of cyborgs before decommissioning them for years now—storing them for study, to see how the process could be improved and the useful life of the units lengthened. Now, those downloaded minds are coming in very useful for new cyborgs that don't have a mind of their own. I like to think of it as a form of recycling."

Below her, the doctors and scientists were removing wires and leads from the cadaver's brand new cranial implants. She flinched as the EKG machine suddenly burst into life with a flurry of beeps before steadying into a normal heart rhythm. As she watched, the corpse's massive chest rose and fell, inflating its lungs with air. Still, the brainwave monitor remained flat, and she could sense no new living mind present around her.

"Welcome to the birth of a new cyborg super-soldier," Jodor said smugly. "He has no living brain to rebel against the technology, causing a malfunction. And we didn't even have to sacrifice an organic soldier to make him. Now, we can use criminals sentenced to execution for their crimes. As long as they're good physical specimens, all we have to do is transport them to this platform before carrying out the sentence, and hand them straight over to the lab techs for processing afterward. Win-win."

In the shadow of the solar array, Pax waited patiently, occasionally tweaking the alignment of the comms antenna in hopes of cleaning up reception a bit more. So far, the only messages had been standard status reports, implying that nothing of import was happening on the orbital station.

"How long does a tour like this normally take?" Kade asked. He didn't look up from his readings, using manual thrusters to keep the fighter from drifting too far away from their cover.

Pax shrugged. "I cannot answer that question. There are far too many variables."

In the time before he was converted, Pax had taken part in his share of official tours as a full Commander in the Ilarian military service. Back then, he had not been equipped to record the passage of time with the electronically enhanced precision he now possessed. He was reasonably certain, however, that the duration varied widely based on the venue and the company.

Before Kade could reply, a new message crackled through the speakers. Pax flicked the switch to record it automatically for later playback, while both he and Kade strained to make sense of it through the static in real time.

"*...this is orbital platform alpha-five requesting...*" The words disappeared into interference. "*... need clarification regarding the security clearance of Vitharan Ambassador Nahleene Veila'ana...*" More static. "*... arrived in the company of Under-Minister Jodor Erisuel, and is currently touring sensitive areas of the station. Please provide guidance on the appropriate response. Captain Tarell out.*"

"Well, son of a bitch," Kade said. "That certainly didn't take long to go tits-up."

Immediately, Pax started running through contingencies. Either the station commander's superiors would instruct him to detain Veila'ana, or they wouldn't. He had no illusions that the Regime would respect her diplomatic immunity, especially if she were suspected of espionage.

If she was detained, they might choose to send her back to the Capital on Jodor Erisuel's ship, or by another means. If they sent her back with the Under-Minister, there was a slim chance he and Kade might be able to disable the unarmed transport and get her away.

They had already discussed the possibility of fleeing through the nearest wormhole gate in an emergency, and going to the abandoned lunar outpost where they'd holed up before. From there, they could escape detection long enough to contact the others and figure out their next move. But all this was only hypothetical until the situation unfolded a bit further.

"*Message received. Please stand by for further orders.*"

Another message came through moments later. *"Captain Tarell. You are ordered to take both the Vitharan ambassador and Under-Minister Erisuel into custody. You will attempt to…"* Static. *"… if the Under-Minister is under duress, or acing of his own free will. Secure the ambassador and return both of them to the Capital complex under guard for further questioning."*

"… And now we're screwed. *Brilliant*," Kade stated bluntly. He sighed and ran a hand roughly over his scalp. "Start plotting a potential intercept course in case they decide to send them planetside in the paper-pusher's ship. That's the only way we'll even have a chance, since it's unarmed. If we're going to get her out, we'll need to hit them just outside the platform's security perimeter. That way it will maximize the amount of time it takes planetary security to get to us."

"Agreed," Pax said, already calculating the optimum trajectory.

Nahleene tamped down her reaction of horror as Jodor continued the tour of the orbital facility. She told herself repeatedly that turning dead bodies into weapons was not materially worse than turning living people into weapons. Somehow, that didn't affect the gut-deep dread she felt as Jodor ushered her into the observation deck above a section of the wheel being used as a training facility.

Below them, a dozen cyborgs were undergoing testing. Seeing them sparring and engaging in physical assessment while her telepathic senses registered only blank space was terrible in a way she couldn't express through words. And yet, that same horror was yet another tactical advantage from the military's perspective. Normal cyborgs already engendered trouser-soiling terror amongst anyone unlucky enough to go up against them in battle. How much more panic would these zombie soldiers cause among the ranks of opposing forces?

This whole program was wrong on so many levels she didn't even know where to start.

One of the zombie cyborgs halted in front of two Vithii men—one wearing a military uniform and another in trainer's clothing— where it stood crisply at attention. The soldier hauled off and unleashed a flurry of blows at the cyborg's face. The thing stood motionless under the assault, except for the tiny movements of its head, snapping back and forth in reaction to the hard punches. After nearly a minute of this abuse, the trainer barked something. The cyborg grabbed its attacker and threw the soldier across the room in a single smooth movement.

Elsewhere, a trainer lined several of the cyborgs up against the wall. Nahleene flinched as he pulled a sidearm and methodically blew a chunk out of each of them, aiming for a different body part every time. The injured subjects didn't so much as blink. Afterward, the trainer directed them to spar in pairs, which they did—ignoring the gaping wounds in their arms, legs, and torsos.

"This is…" Nahleene whispered, not sure how she planned on ending the sentence.

"This is the future of warfare," Jodor said, clearly relishing her shocked reaction.

She shook her head slowly, not wanting to think about a future where ships full of these…

things... might pour into Maelfian orbit—shock troops to decimate a peaceful world. Before she could recover enough to play her role as impartial diplomatic observer, the lift doors opened behind her. She turned, aware that she must be as pale and waxy looking as the reanimated soldiers in the bay below.

Captain Tarell strode into the observation room, flanked by two of the dead-eyed cyborgs. "Guards," he said, addressing the two men who had been acting as their escorts during the tour, "restrain the Ambassador and the Under-Minister. They are both under arrest."

Jodor squawked something in outrage as the soldier nearest to him grabbed him by the arm and drew his sidearm. Nahleene reacted instinctively when the other one did the same to her. It was a stupid miscalculation, she realized a moment too late, but the instant the guard touched the bare skin of her arm, she hit him with a powerful wave of exhaustion. He staggered back and crumpled to the ground, insensible.

She heard Jodor gasp, and Tarell barked, "Unit X-41, restrain the woman!"

The cyborg at Tarell's left shoulder marched forward, and Nahleene scrambled backward. There was nowhere to go. Her back hit the clearsteel viewport, and the creature took the opportunity to snatch her arm with a movement so fast she barely registered it.

Its grip was clammy, and there was no living presence behind it. Her skin crawled beneath its touch. Out of desperation, she pushed emotion at it anyway, but there was no indication that the thing even registered the attempt. It dragged her forward with a grip as strong as a steel band, and she went still and quiet in its grasp like the trapped prey animal she was—eyes wide and frightened, heart racing as though it would try to pound free of her chest.

Jodor's eyes darted back and forth between the collapsed guard and Nahleene's face, clarity returning to his gaze, followed by rage. He raised his free arm to point at her with a shaking finger.

"That's... she's..." He looked at the downed soldier again. "That's what she did to me! The bitch is a telepath! *She's using mind control!*"

SEVEN

Right now, Nahleene didn't even feel like she had control of her *own* mind, much less someone else's. She needed to protest... needed to come up with some reasonable explanation for the guard she'd overpowered. But all she could feel was panic at being held by the walking cadaver that still gripped her arm impassively.

Tarell was giving her a shrewd look, and she cursed the fact that he clearly wasn't an idiot. He must have checked up on her after she and Jodor left to tour the station; gotten guidance from his superiors planetside. *Shit*. She needed to get herself together *right the fuck now*, or this was going to turn into a complete disaster.

"Are you a touch telepath, Ambassador?" Tarell asked. "I'm certain such a fact should be listed in your file, if so."

"I have no idea what you're talking about," she managed, despite the evidence to the contrary lying at her feet, snoring softly. "The Under-Minister invited me on a tour of the station when he learned I was interested in the cyborg project. He started acting rather oddly during the journey here. A bit... confused, but only off and on. Perhaps he should undergo a medical check when we return to the Capital?"

She was stalling, and not very well. Frankly, she didn't see a way out of this. Which had always been a possibility, but she'd stupidly discounted the likelihood that the station commander would act so quickly and decisively. Not when she had Jodor's presence here to act as camouflage for the visit.

"*Confused?*" Jodor snapped, clearly incensed now that her influence over him had dissipated. "How dare you!" He gestured at her a bit wildly. "I'm a victim of this... this... *outworlder*! She's clearly a spy—"

Well spotted. Ten points to the attempted murderer, she thought grimly.

Tarell cut off Jodor's tirade. "You will both undergo brain scans to confirm your mental states. Ambassador, if the Under-Minister's accusations prove true, you will be rendered safe, and afterward, both of you will be returned to the Capital under guard."

Nahleene blanched, wondering what he meant by 'rendered safe.'

"I am a diplomat from a treaty world, with full immunity from detainment and prosecution," she said.

"You'll have to take that up with law enforcement," Tarell replied coldly. "My only concern is the security of this installation, which has clearly been compromised. Guards, take these two to medical, and someone get this soldier out of here." He swept his hand carelessly toward the figure on the floor.

The cyborg holding Nahleene dragged her unceremoniously into the lift. She stumbled, only the thing's immense strength keeping her upright. The Vithii guard followed with Jodor in tow.

"You conniving hag," he hissed. "You've been a spy from the start. I should have known! You'll pay for what you've done to me..."

Listening to the waste of space standing next to her was just about the last thing Nahleene needed right now. She glared at him.

"Careful, *Under-Minister.* Or I might suddenly remember what you tried to do to your bondmate in the prison infirmary a week ago."

Jodor paled momentarily before his expression turned even angrier than before. He did, however, shut the fuck up—so that was something. The Vithii guard glanced between them curiously. The cyborg, unsurprisingly, showed no reaction.

The rest of the trip was made in tense silence. Nahleene's mind spun in circles, trying and failing to come up with any way out of the situation. They arrived at the medical bay, where the Vithii guard reported to a cold-eyed woman in a lab coat.

"Captain Tarell ordered these prisoners delivered here, Doctor."

That chilly gaze clearly belonged to someone who had no problem turning sentient beings—alive or dead—into mindless weapons. That gaze raked over Nahleene, and she shivered.

"Yes," replied the doctor. "He called ahead. Cyborg—take the woman into the scanning bay. Do not allow her to get close enough to anyone to touch them.

Shit, what did they think she was going to do? Put every single person on the platform to sleep?

The cyborg manhandled her into another room. She was appalled to see that the scanning table had manacles attached. Of course... they brought prisoners here for cyborg conversion. No doubt most of them were less than cooperative subjects when it came to testing before their impending executions.

"I demand to speak to the Vitharan consulate!" she cried, and was ignored.

She might as well have been a ragdoll as far as her captor was concerned. The cyborg hefted her onto the table and ignored her struggles as it forced her left arm into a metal cuff, and then her right. Her ankles followed, and finally a band tightened around her neck. She could feel her panicked pulse throbbing against the constricting metal.

"*I do not consent to this scan!*" she choked out, still to no effect.

The cold-eyed doctor approached, attaching electrodes to Nahleene's forehead—taking great care not to touch her directly while doing so. The woman didn't meet her eyes, giving her about as much consideration as she probably gave the corpses she and her colleagues converted into cyborgs.

Nahleene couldn't see where Jodor had been taken, but Captain Tarell entered the room, his gaze flicking carelessly over her body manacled to the table. He turned his attention to the cyborg, which was out of her line of sight.

"Unit X-41. When the medical personnel are done with the detainees, you will accompany Lieutenant Raithern to return them to the Capital on board the Under-Minister's transport. For the duration of this mission, you will follow the lieutenant's orders in all things."

"Understood," the cyborg rasped in a flat, lifeless voice.

Nahleene shuddered against the cold metal table, but a tiny sliver of hope ran through her. If she could somehow influence the Vithii lieutenant, she could control both of them as long as the cyborg followed his orders. Maybe then she could get away, or at least contact Pax and Kade for help. She just had to play it cool until she got a chance to touch him... try to lull them all into a false sense of security.

"Everyone please stand back," the doctor said, having finished attaching wires and electrodes to Nahleene's skin.

A moment later, a red beam played over her body from head to toe, and back again. Nahleene held her breath, hoping against hope that the Ilarian tech wouldn't be able to make sense of her hybrid brain. That hope was dashed a few minutes later, when the doctor looked up from her readouts.

"Scans show brain activity off the scales in the parahippocampus," she reported. "The subject is a powerful telepath. Gene analysis is consistent with a lab-assisted Vitharan/Maelfian hybrid."

Nahleene closed her eyes in defeat.

Heavy footsteps approached, and Captain Tarell's voice came from close by when he spoke. She didn't open her eyes to look at him.

"Very well," he said. "Sedate her and do whatever is necessary to render her harmless for transport."

At that, her eyes *did* fly open. "No!" she said. "No sedation! I do not consent—"

A hypo-injector hissed against her neck, just below the metal band restraining her head. Sudden vertigo blurred her vision.

"I... I do not... c-cons..."

The dizziness chased her down into oblivion a few seconds later.

Two-point-one-seven cycles after he and Kade intercepted the final message from the station's commander acknowledging his orders to detain the ambassador and the Under-Minister, the docking lights above the little transport vessel flashed into life.

"Standby," Pax warned.

Kade straightened in his seat. "I see it."

Immediately, he started to power up the fighter's systems, most of which had been on standby to conserve fuel while they focused everything on monitoring the comm channels. Pax twisted in the cramped space, reaching for the weapons locker. Kade always kept it well stocked, and he strapped on everything that he could carry without hampering his ability to squeeze through the fighter's tiny docking chute.

"Do you have specs on file for that model of orbital transport?" Kade asked.

"Yes," Pax told him, settling back into the copilot's seat. "I'll attempt to disable the engines without compromising hull integrity or life support."

Kade gave a short nod and flicked a switch. "You have weapons control. Of course, the downside of this plan is that once we dock, any guards who are along for the ride will have their weapons trained on the airlock door the moment you try to board."

Pax shrugged. Anything he might do to disable the guards before he boarded the ship also risked Veila'ana's wellbeing. And it wouldn't exactly be the first time he'd led an assault on an airlock with hostile forces waiting on the other side.

"As long as you can get us docked with the transport. I'll take it from there," he said.

Kade eyed him with a sour expression. "Sure, no problem. What's that human saying? 'Piece of pie'?"

"Cake," Pax corrected absently. In the distance, movement drew his enhanced senses back to full alert. "They're underway."

"Right," Kade acknowledged. "Count it down for me. I don't want to leave the cover of the solar array until the last possible moment, and it's still interfering with my sensors."

"On it," Pax said, eyeing the ship's progress as it maneuvered to a new heading and started toward the planet. He followed it for several seconds, judging its speed and distance from them. "Engage engines in five… four… three… two… one… now."

The sleek fighter roared into life, following the preset intercept course he'd prepared earlier. Kade brought the sensors back online and studied them, making tiny corrections to hurtle them toward a rendezvous with the orbital transport's trajectory. As they'd intended, the transport had just exited the platform's defined security perimeter when whoever was flying it detected their approach. The craft immediately undertook evasive maneuvers, and a distress call followed within seconds. However, the ship's position outside of the space controlled by the orbital platform meant the message would be automatically routed planetside, even though it would take longer to scramble a response from the surface.

Kade muttered something uncomplimentary and changed course to compensate for the transport's evasion tactics. Meanwhile, Pax focused on aiming the fighter's phase cannons at a vulnerable point below the ship's exhaust port. He needed a tight, controlled burst that would catastrophically damage the ion engines without penetrating the pressurized sections of the interior. There would only be one opportunity to make the shot.

"Twelve hundred klicks and closing," Kade reported. The transport swerved again and he altered course to mirror them. "Eleven hundred. One thousand. Nine hundred. Seven hundred. Five hundred. Accelerating to attack speed. Two hundred. One hundred. Fifty. Coming within weapons range... *now*."

Pax fired a controlled burst of phased energy at the port the instant before Kade peeled the fighter away. A flare of red and orange erupted from the back of the transport, followed by a trail of vaporous particles, glittering in the reflected light from the planet below. The ship slewed and settled into a slow spin.

"Fuck," Kade said. "Give me a minute to compensate for the spin. This is gonna be a serious pain in the ass for docking..."

Pax secured the weapons system and unbuckled himself from the copilot's seat. As Kade matched the fighter's trajectory to the disabled ship's slow spiraling freefall, He moved to the top of the docking chute and checked the safeties on the sidearms he was carrying.

"Didn't realize I was going to need a godsdamned anti-nausea injection for this mission," Kade groused as the stars and planetary surface spun lazily around them, visible through the clearsteel cockpit. "All right. Grab onto something. Docking port contact in three... two... one..."

Pax placed a hand on the edge of the chute, and a solid clank of metal against metal rocked the fighter.

"Bet that'll leave a scratch," Kade muttered. A series of softer clunks followed, and he breathed out harshly. "Docking clamps engaged. Your turn, now. Hurry back, and don't fucking well get yourself killed."

Pax nodded acknowledgment and descended the three-meter long chute that led through the fighter's belly to the external docking port. At the bottom, he slapped the control to engage the interior airlock seal, so the fighter wouldn't depressurize on the off chance that the interior of the transport had lost atmosphere during the attack.

On the other side of the port in front of him waited one or more guards, no doubt with weapons trained on their side of the door. With the fighter airlock sealed behind him, Pax set himself to one side of the small space and slapped a hand over the control, a flash-bang grenade held at the ready in his other hand. Either the guards had opened the door on their side and would charge him with weapons blazing, or they'd kept it sealed and locked in hopes of slowing him down.

The fighter's door whooshed aside to reveal the transport's door closed tight. Still keeping to the side, Pax exchanged the grenade for a laser pistol and used the beam to bore a small hole through the area above the port's locking mechanism. He jammed a micro-explosive charge into the red-hot space, plastered himself against the wall next to the door, and thumbed the remote detonator on his belt. The small explosion destroyed the locking latch, and the circular door rolled open a few inches.

Pax pulled the pin on the flash-bang and tossed it through an instant before blaster beams started flying through the small gap, hitting the far wall of the airlock. Two seconds later, sound and light erupted inside, and the beams stopped. With a burst of controlled strength, Pax jerked the port the rest of the way open and charged inside, blaster drawn.

A Vithii guard was struggling to his knees, his weapon still clutched in his hand. Pax shot a smoking hole through his chest and he fell back, unmoving. A blur of motion at his right preceded a heavy weight tackling him to the deck. It was too strong and too fast to be a meatbag, he realized immediately. Pax rolled and jammed a knee up, trying to throw his attacker off. Hands clung to him like magnetic clamps; limbs at least as strong as his own wrestling him back down to the floor and pinning him.

Metallic implants flashed, but the eyes in the face of the cyborg looking down at him were not merely emotionless—they were dead. No consciousness lay behind that lifeless gaze, and part of Pax's mind scrambled to place the realization within some kind of context. The rest was intent on the fight, and it quickly became clear that he was outclassed. He freed a hand to grab for another weapon, but the unknown cyborg unit merely knocked it out of his grip.

It had apparently lost its own weapon during the flash-bang grenade's explosion. Now, it reached for the compact blaster hooked on Pax's belt. Pax shot a hand out, grabbing its wrist. Cyber-enhanced muscle strained against cyber-enhanced muscle, Pax slowly losing ground as his opponent bore down on him.

Running through possible strategies, Pax altered course and yanked the cyborg's arm toward the deck instead of trying to push it away. At the same time, he rolled again, this time managing to dislodge his attacker and get free. He lunged for the same blaster the cyborg had tried to take from him and got off a single shot before it tackled him again. The thing was fast—the beam missed its heart and tore a small hole through its side, instead.

Pax felt ribs crack as he was slammed into the wall, and the cyborg immediately went for the weapon again. Once his attacker managed to control the blaster, Pax knew the fight would end… and not in his favor. He threw the blaster as far away as he could, and turned his focus inward, to the software systems that wound through his organic brain.

Query: connect? Pax sent.

The cyborg struggling with him stilled.

Security check: password, came the silent, electronic reply.

Pax stilled as well, concentrating his complete attention on the connection.

Password override. Emergency protocol alpha-one-beta-three. Delineate current chain of mission command, Pax ordered.

The cyborg's dead eyes blinked as his system registered the protocol.

Raithern, Thiellus. Lieutenant, Second Class, it replied.

Good. There was only one commanding officer present.

Status of Raithern, Thiellus, Lieutenant, Second Class? Pax asked.

The cyborg paused, scanning its surroundings.

Deceased, it reported.

Pax stared into that blank visage, still trying to integrate the reality of its existence into his worldview.

Accept new entry re: chain of command. Unit PX-12, Commander, serial number 43-298-412. Authorization red-alpha.

A pause. Another blink.

Entry accepted, said the cyborg.

Pax let his muscles unlock.

Stand down. Enter power-saving mode, he told it.

Without a word, the other cyborg released its grip and stepped back. Pax moved away from the bulkhead where he'd been pinned and picked up the nearest discarded blaster—moving a bit stiffly as the bots in his bloodstream rushed to repair his broken ribs. He turned and blew a hole through the cyborg's head. It fell, and he fired a second shot through its heart, just to be safe.

Turning his back on the dead guards, he scanned the rest of the ship. It was not a large vessel, and he could detect two more life forms—one with a racing pulse and heavy breathing in the cabin that housed the flight controls, and another located aft, its heartbeat far too slow and steady to indicate consciousness, given the current stressful situation. He headed for the flight control cabin first.

The door was locked, but flimsy. He blasted the controls and shoved it open. Inside, Under-Minister Jodor Erisuel stood braced with his back against the forward control panel, a stunner held in his shaking hand. Evidently the guard had allowed him a defensive weapon during the attack, though what good he thought it would do against something that had already managed to get past a military cyborg was an open question.

"Stay back," Erisuel barked, and fired.

Pax was already sidestepping the instant he saw the Under-Minister's finger twitch, and the beam passed harmlessly by his shoulder. An instant later, the tiny sidearm crumpled in Pax's grip, and he threw it aside. The Vithii bureaucrat tried to shrink back even farther, but there was nowhere to go. Pax grabbed him by the shirtfront and lifted him effortlessly until his feet flailed above the deck.

"Jodor Erisuel," he said, staring into the terrified, bugging eyes in front of him, "thank you for the actions which resulted in my acquaintance with your estranged bondmate. Your cruelty and cowardice toward her has indirectly provided invaluable support to both myself and my comrades."

Jodor scrabbled ineffectually at Pax's wrist, his breath coming in harsh gasps as he rasped, "What... are you... saying?"

"I am saying goodbye," Pax said, and shot him through the chest. The body dropped to the deck in a crumpled heap, and Pax went to retrieve Veila'ana from the aft compartment.

EIGHT

As expected, the ambassador was unconscious, strapped onto a medical cot inside the tiny utility area. An unidentified implant was embedded in her right temple, the skin around it raw and red. There was no time to investigate it, however, so he merely unstrapped her and lifted her slight form into his arms. They needed to move; no doubt planetary security was already scrambling, ready to head their way.

Pax squeezed through the damaged airlock port with his burden and sealed the hatch on the fighter's side. Once it was closed, he opened the interior hatch.

"Kade," he called, easing into the cramped docking chute with Veila'ana pressed close against his front so they would both fit.

Kade's upper body appeared at the other end of the tube. Pax handed Veila'ana's unresponsive form up to him, and he pulled her into the cockpit. Pax followed and stripped off his remaining weapons. Kade had already settled the ambassador in the copilot's seat and was checking her pulse.

"Other survivors?" he asked. "And what the hell is this tech on her temple?"

"No survivors," Pax said shortly. "And I do not know."

"All right. No time." Kade settled back into the pilot's seat, checking the airlock seals and releasing the docking clamps. "I'm vaporizing that transport, and then we'll make a run for it."

The docking clamps fell away with a series of thumps, and Pax hesitated, looking at the figure occupying the only other seat in the fighter.

Kade's eyes flicked up at him. "Stop gawping. We need to move. Just sit the fuck down and hold onto her for the jump."

With few other options, Pax eased Veila'ana into his arms and sat, arranging her so she was curled in his lap. The seat restraints would not accommodate both of them, but he was confident he could steady her during any sort of normal turbulence.

Kade righted the fighter from its tumble. They jetted away from the drifting transport, and he positioned them a few hundred meters from the hulk. A moment later, twin torpedoes shot from the belly of the small ship, and the transport exploded into an expanding sphere of dust and gas. Kade didn't wait around to appreciate his handiwork. The fighter hurtled away, racing for the nearest wormhole gate.

Pax reached around Veila'ana to activate his sensor panel, steadying her head against his shoulder as he did so. "Half a dozen security fighters approaching from the planet's surface," he reported. "Attack formation."

"I see them," Kade muttered. "Hang on—this might get bumpy." The fighter screamed through the wormhole gate just as the first blasts from their pursuers' weapons streaked past them. "Now for the interesting part. Can you ready the engines for subspace transition?"

"Yes," Pax said, inputting the parameters one-handed.

The wormhole system was designed to have discrete entry and exit points scattered around the local cluster. Of course, no system that large and complex was without flaws, and there were several places where the subspace barriers around the tunnel were weak. Any smuggler or criminal worth their salt knew that if you could match your engine frequency and amplitude to the frequency and amplitude of a weak spot in the barrier, you could force a ship through the wall of the tunnel and bypass the gates, which were always monitored. Such passage left no trace afterward. The only clue was the existence of the weak spot itself, and it took time to detect such things inside the vastness of the system.

Pax and his friends had utilized this particular weak spot to great advantage for the span of several months, using it as a back door to get to and from an abandoned stellar cartography outpost on an unremarkable moon located around one of the outer planets of the Ilarian system. They had abandoned that outpost as a tactical decision after Skye crashed there while fleeing Regime forces. But now, weeks later, it was their best chance for escape and concealment, at least on a temporary basis.

"We're coming up on the weak spot," Kade said tightly.

"Engines ready," Pax reported. "Intermix ratios under your control."

"Hold onto our passenger," said the other man. "I'll try not to bash us around too badly."

Pax checked the sensors one last time. Kade's fighter was fast, and the pursuing ships were still some distance behind them. Too far away to make sense of the garbled readings they would get as the fighter ahead of them burst through the tunnel wall. Their pursuers would continue blindly on to the next gate, only to find that the ship they were chasing had disappeared without a trace.

Kade hit the intermix control, and the engines' smooth purr grew into a rough growl. The fighter veered toward the subspace barrier, shuddering as it made contact and forced its way through. The violent vibrations were enough to make Pax's teeth clatter inside his skull. He steadied Veila'ana with a strong grip around her shoulders, her soft body pressed to his.

The jostling lasted for several seconds, only to stop abruptly as the ship emerged into normal space, engines still sputtering. Kade slapped a hand over the intermix controls, realigning the mixture until the growl smoothed back into its normal hum. He checked the sensors immediately afterward.

"We lost them," he noted. "Let's get this bird down and docked, so we can try to contact the others."

The old lunar outpost appeared to be in exactly the same condition as they had left it. The crashed shuttle had not been disturbed, indicating that Ilarian security forces had not been successful in tracing Skye here. They'd put the station in standby mode before they left. Once Kade set them down next to the umbilical port, Pax eased Veila'ana off his lap so he could complete the docking procedure and check the station's interior.

Oxygen levels were low, so he unlocked the controls and started up the secondary generators. Within a few minutes, the levels crept up to normal range. The heaters would take longer to bring the temperature up from standby levels, but the current temperature was not dangerous for Vithii—merely uncomfortable. He returned to the fighter to report the conditions.

The medical bay had been outdated and poorly stocked when they'd first found the outpost, but Ryder had improved it over the months they'd spent here. It was there that Pax took Veila'ana, placing her on the same cot where Ryder had operated on Skye's battered body after the shuttle crash, using some of Pax's own bots to save her life.

"You okay here?" Kade asked gruffly.

Pax shook his head. "I have her. See if you can contact Ryder. We may need her for whatever this implant is."

Kade nodded brusquely. "I'll keep you posted."

After he left, Pax turned his attention to the medbay systems, rebooting everything and running status checks. It was somewhat worrisome that the ambassador had not shown any sign of waking, not even during the attack on the transport and the juddering transition through the weak spot in the wormhole's subspace barrier. With all medical systems showing ready, he started a full body scan.

The results scrolled across the display screen. Vitals were on the low end of normal for a Vithii, but the results would be complicated by the ambassador's hybrid parentage and the gene manipulation she'd undergone. As Pax had suspected, the implant showed sign of nanotech activity, and it had infiltrated her brain tissue around the parahippocampus region. However, he could only guess at its function in the absence of hard data.

Drug scans flagged the presence of a common sedative in her bloodstream, which might or might not be enough to account for her continued unresponsiveness. On the one hand, Pax was loath to attempt waking her without knowing more about the cranial implant, but on the other hand, he would gain no more useful data about the thing's effects while she was unconscious. Hunter's fighter was still at the safehouse on Ilarius' southern continent, and Pax had no doubt that he would use it to ferry Ryder here as soon as he could. When she arrived, she would need as much information as possible about Veila'ana's condition.

Mind made up, Pax called up all relevant data about the sedative and its effects. The drug used for its reversal was stocked in Ryder's meticulously organized storage cabinet. He checked the expiration date and dosage on the package, and was preparing a hypo-injector when Kade returned.

"Hunter's bringing Ryder here as soon as he can get the fighter prepped and airborne," he said. "The others will follow, but they'll need to find alternate transport, obviously. Still no luck reaching Ash, but I left a message via the usual channels." He jerked his chin toward the cot. "What do the scans show?"

"She is sedated. The implant contains nanotech and is infiltrating her brain tissue. Otherwise, there is no sign of injury."

Kade raised a brow. "That's a pretty big 'otherwise'."

"I intend to reverse the effects of the sedation in hopes of learning more about her condition before Ryder arrives," Pax continued.

"Risky," Kade observed.

Pax readied the injection. "The risk will only become greater, the longer the implant continues to grow into her brain."

"And we still don't know what, if anything, she was able to find out before she was captured," Kade conceded.

After his run-in with the cyborg that wasn't a proper cyborg, Pax had some very unpleasant theories—but right now, only Veila'ana could confirm them. "If she can communicate, she may be able to shed light on the subject," he agreed.

He carefully injected the contents of the hypo into a vein in the ambassador's neck, and set the instrument aside for later sterilization. For approximately ninety seconds, there was no reaction. Then, Veila'ana's pulse rate increased, and her eyes began to dart from side to side beneath her closed lids, as though she were dreaming. Pax moved to stand next to the medical cot, while Kade looked on with interest from a few steps away.

"Ambassador?" Pax prompted, watching the brain activity monitors for a reaction. Belatedly, he remembered Veila'ana's directive in the club, when she'd asked them to use her given name. "Nahleene?"

———◆———

Nahleene gradually became aware of a terrible ache in her skull, throbbing in time with her heartbeat. It felt like someone had stabbed a knife into her brain, and was twisting it back and forth relentlessly. She struggled to remember what had happened to her... to figure out where she was and what was going on around her. Her thought processes were muddled, like she was caught partway between dreams and the waking world, unable to grasp either reality.

A voice penetrated the layer of red mist, its raspy timbre odd, but somehow familiar.

"Ambassador?" silence reigned for a beat before the same voice asked, "Nahleene?"

A wisp of memory wafted up.

"Seeing as how I've been poking around in your minds, you both might as well call me Nahleene. It seems silly to stand on ceremony at this point."

Bits of the past few days started to filter in. Ryder contacting her. Meeting with Pax and Kade. Arranging to do... something. Something that she shouldn't have done. Something that would get her in trouble with both the Vitharan government and her Maelfian handlers.

The voice belonged to Pax. Why couldn't she feel his presence nearby? Was he speaking to her through a comm unit? The pain in her head ratcheted up. She needed to open her eyes. Figure out where she was. Why she was alone. She could find the comm controls... reply to Pax. Find out what was going on. Had she been hit on the head? Was that why she couldn't seem to think straight?

She whimpered at the prospect of opening her eyes when her head hurt this badly... a pathetic sound that made her glad she was alone. Gritting her teeth, she peeled sticky eyelids up. The lights were dim, thank all that was holy, but she couldn't see a thing except for nebulous blurs. She blinked several times, trying to clear her vision, and nearly fell off whatever she was lying on in surprise when one of the blurs moved. Fresh pain stabbed into her after the sudden movement, drawing a gasp from her throat. Surprise turned to panic when a hand gripped her upper arm, steadying her.

There was... no one there. Someone was looming over her. *Touching* her. But... she couldn't *feel* him. *What*—?

"Remain calm," said the voice that sounded like Pax, but wasn't. "You are in a safe place. Can you speak?"

The jolt of adrenaline cleared her vision enough for her to make out her surroundings more clearly, though it did nothing to ease the debilitating pain in her skull. The apparition holding her arm did indeed look exactly like her memory of Pax, but that memory blurred with other wavering visions of towering creatures that her mind couldn't sense.

"No," she moaned, sudden desperation lending her the strength to claw herself into a sitting position, reaching for the specter's face. "No... this is wrong. Where are you? *What* are you?"

Her hand found warm flesh that felt real, but there was nothing beyond it—no hum of a living mind, cyber-enhanced or otherwise. Only blankness. More movement at the corner of her eye drew her terrified gaze, and she saw a second figure coming toward her. This one looked exactly like Kade, but again, it was a phantom. Empty.

"Nahleene?" Pax's voice again. A hand grasped her wrist in a gentle grip and moved her fingertips away from the empty flesh they'd been resting against.

Still, there was nothing. Two realities fought for dominance—the one her eyes told her was real, and the one her telepathic senses insisted was real. A sudden awareness washed through her of being utterly and completely alone, cut off from the living world while ghosts gathered around her.

The pain in her skull brought tears to her eyes. Even so, she stared as if transfixed at the storm-blue gaze holding hers... a gaze that promised life and safety, but held only the emptiness of death behind it. Giving into the terror of this twisted half-world into which she had awakened, Nahleene opened her mouth, drew in a harsh breath, and screamed.

NINE

Nahleene screamed and thrashed in Pax's light grip, obviously having little idea of where she was or what was happening. He restrained her as gently as he could, aware that his decision to bring her out of sedation had been in error.

"Kade," he said, pitching his voice loud enough to be heard over the ambassador's agonized shrieks, "prepare five milliliters of Iodrazine. Quickly."

Kade returned a tight nod and crossed to the drug storage unit in two long strides, coming up a moment later with the required injection. Confident that Kade had more experience with hypos than anyone else he knew with the possible exception of Ryder, Pax did not reach for the little injector he held. Instead, he held Nahleene's body trapped against his with one arm, and used his other hand to steady her thrashing head against his shoulder as she continued to wail.

Kade's mouth was a grim line as he efficiently positioned the head of the pressure injector over the same vein Pax had used earlier to inject the sedative's antagonist.

"We're sedating you," Kade said. "We have a doctor coming soon."

"Until then, we will keep you safe," Pax added, unsure if she could understand their words at all. "Ryder will determine what is wrong and fix it."

There was no indication she'd even heard him. Gradually, her cries and struggles subsided until she was once more unconscious. Pax eased her back to lie against the cot, and Kade ran a shaky hand through his hair.

"That was... unproductive," Pax said.

The look Kade shot him was disbelieving, but after a moment he shook his head. "I suppose we should be glad that whatever's wrong with her didn't transmit itself to you, after she knocked you on your ass the other night. Small blessings."

Pax blinked as the words registered.

"I did not experience any bleed-through of her distraught emotional state, even when she touched my face," he said slowly.

Kade shrugged. "Yeah? Like I said, that's just as well."

Pax met his eyes. "You misunderstand. She was clearly attempting to make mental contact when she touched me. But I felt nothing."

Understanding dawned in Kade's expression. "You think she didn't either? Because of the implant?"

Pax's brow furrowed. "I suppose it would be emotionally disconcerting for a lifelong telepath to awaken in unfamiliar surroundings, and without any mental awareness."

Kade blew out a breath. "I imagine it would, at that. No way to know for certain with her out cold, but I guess I can see why the goons on the station might want to neuter her mental powers before trying to transport her. I wonder how many of them she took out before they got her?"

"They would certainly have access to the doctors and the tech to implant such a device, should they wish to do so." Pax mused. He looked down at the pale form on the bed. She looked... small. Defenseless. He realized, rather nonsensically, that he'd missed the jolt of secondhand emotion when she'd touched him—even if that emotion was distress.

"Well... it's a decent working theory, if nothing else," Kade said. "Ryder will have to confirm it when she gets here, or not."

Pax ran a quick gaze over Kade, aware of the passage of time and the faint tremor still visible in the other man's hands. "You are due for another dose of neurotonin," he said absently.

Kade narrowed his eyes. "Do you think? Fuck off, Pax. If you want to play nursemaid, do it with her." He jerked his chin at Veila'ana.

Pax ignored the abuse. "Do you have a sufficient amount for the likely duration of our stay?"

He could hear Kade's teeth grind together. "I've been doing this for a very long time. There's more than a week's supply in the stasis cabinet in my old quarters."

Pax waited, sensing that there was more.

"Though..." Kade paused, his jaw clenching even tighter, "... if you could go transfer the doses into the time-release safe and bring me one to use now, that might be... better... than if I tried to do it myself right now. With... the cravings."

"Of course," Pax said. "Keep an eye on her vitals. I will return shortly."

———◆———

Ryder and Hunter arrived some three cycles later, docking at one of the outpost's secondary ports. As was her usual habit, Ryder was all business the moment she stepped through the airlock.

"What's her current status?" she asked Pax without preamble, barely slowing down in her purposeful march toward the medical bay.

Pax put out a gentle hand, grasping her shoulder and bringing her to a momentary halt. Ryder jumped a bit at the contact, still unused to the idea of letting any of them touch her. She seemed to waver for a moment between bristling or allowing the familiarity, before she consciously relaxed her muscles and took a breath.

"Greetings, Ryder," he said, a tiny bit pointedly. "Thank you for coming so quickly."

Pax caught the nearly imperceptible twitch of a smile on Hunter's lips, quickly covered. Ryder seemed on the verge of sputtering, but she caught herself and shot him a wry glance instead.

"Hello, Pax," she said, laying on enough irony to make it clear she was still the same prickly hardass she'd always been, and was only humoring him by subjecting herself to social niceties. "Good to see you and Kade managed to stay in one piece, even if Veila'ana seems to have acquired some extra pieces along the way. Now, answer the bloody question. What's her status?"

Pax fell into step beside her as they resumed the journey to the medbay. "She is currently sedated with five milliliters of Iodrazine, administered three-point-two cycles ago. I attempted to rouse her from sedation shortly after we arrived, but she immediately became agitated. While I cannot confirm it, she appeared to have lost her telepathic abilities, or had them muffled in some way. The lack of mental feedback seemed quite distressing to her. I sedated her again for her own safety."

Ryder's lips twisted with displeasure. "So, a cranial implant that appears to be interfering with her telepathy?" she asked. "Does it contain nanotech?"

"Yes," Pax confirmed. "There would have been several doctors and technicians on the orbital platform qualified to implant such a device, and ample access to the necessary technology."

She nodded grimly. "Okay. I need to see the scans, but then I'll want to program some of your bots to deactivate and reverse whatever process they used to attack or alter her brain tissue. This is going to take a while to undo. I won't just start hacking into her skull with a protoplaser as long as there's a chance to fix the damage on a microscopic level instead."

"I agree that would be preferable," Pax agreed. "There are several questions about the cyborg program that only the ambassador can answer. I encountered a cyborg during Ambassador Veila'ana's retrieval that… utilized an unfamiliar version of the technology. The implications of what I saw are potentially alarming."

"One crisis at a time, please," Ryder said sharply.

The door to the medical bay whooshed open, and Kade looked up from the monitoring equipment. He tipped his head in greeting at Ryder and Hunter, and pushed upright from the corner of the console he'd been perched against.

"No change in the patient," he said, moving out of Ryder's way as she approached the console with single-minded purpose. "I assume you want the rest of us out from underfoot?"

"Not Pax," she said absently. "But you two, yes."

"Well, *tei'laal*," said Kade, "I guess it's clear when we're not wanted. Come give me a hand with one of the generators. The thing sounds like it's on its last legs. You and I can play machine-mechanic while these two play flesh-mechanic."

"It's no worse than re-tuning the engine on a fifty-year-old agricultural harvester, I suppose," Hunter agreed easily, standing aside to let Kade precede him through the door. He paused, looking back at Pax. "We were able to reach Ash, by the way. He wasn't happy about it, but he agreed to shuttle the others here with the stolen courier ship he's been hiding in one of Kade's hangars. They should arrive within the next seven cycles or so."

"Understood," Pax said. "Station sensors are online and tied into my systems. Let me know when you're ready to return to a standard watch rotation."

Hunter gave a nod of acknowledgement and followed Kade out, leaving Pax alone with Ryder and Veila'ana. He watched the ambassador's pale face as Ryder disappeared into the side room to put on sterile scrubs and prep for microsurgery. Even heavily sedated, a furrow marred Veila'ana's forehead, as though she were confused or worried.

A few minutes later, Ryder emerged and raised a sharp eyebrow at him. "All right, Pax. Give me some blood for a bot harvest, and let's get this party started."

Eight-point-four cycles later, Pax emerged from the medical room, having been shooed away once Ryder confirmed that his donated bots were replicating properly and carrying out their programmed instructions as expected. It would take several cycles more before it became clear whether or not they were able to overcome and reverse the programming of the nanotech already present in Veila'ana's brain, and even more time to complete the process so the cranial implant could be safely removed.

The others had arrived safely about a cycle earlier. Pax had tied his systems into the outpost's systems remotely, and passed the alert on to Hunter when the courier ship had approached their perimeter. He was confident that if anything had been amiss, either Hunter or Kade would have contacted him to let him know.

He, in turn, made a succinct report to Hunter about Ryder's progress and the expected timeline going forward. Then, he headed for the small equipment storage bay that the others had converted into a workout room, to find out why the outpost's internal sensors registered a single Vithii male with an unusually elevated heart rate and body temperature inside.

His enhanced hearing picked up the sound of grievous bodily injury being done to an unarmed punching bag while he was still twenty paces from the door. With Hunter accounted for and Kade not prone to bouts of sudden boxing practice in moments of stress, the process of elimination left Draven as the likely culprit. There were a limited number of reasons why Draven might feel the urgent need to hit something, and Pax spared a moment to wonder if Hunter had failed to notify him of important information after all.

The door was closed but not locked, and it squealed open on rusty tracks at his approach. Inside, Draven was bared to the waist, his knuckles taped hastily enough that one of the pieces was starting to come loose as he pummeled the cylindrical heavy bag hanging from a durasteel strut in the ceiling. Droplets of sweat spattered from his face and body with every punch, and he was so focused on whatever internal battle he was waging that he hadn't noticed the screech of the door.

Even during a relatively stable situation in friendly territory, that was sub-optimal.

"Draven," Pax said, projecting his voice loudly enough to be heard over the flurry of dull thuds echoing around the room.

Draven whirled, his right fist cocked for a blow—clearly taken by surprise and still only partially aware of his surroundings. Rage clouded his normally pleasant features, his copper eyes snapping fire, lips drawn back from bared teeth. Pax raised an eyebrow at him.

A pause, a blink, and Pax could practically see him recalling himself to the present. Draven looked at the bag; looked down at his hands where the tape was unraveling from around his bruised knuckles.

"Is there a problem I should know about?" Pax asked mildly.

Draven's chest was rising and falling like a bellows. Perspiration still dripped off of him. It took him another ten seconds to compose himself enough to offer a reply.

"He's going to get himself killed," he said eventually, and then appeared surprised at the hoarse way his voice emerged.

There was little question as to the identity of the 'he' in question.

"Yes," Pax agreed. "It seems increasingly possible."

Draven took an actual, physical step backward, as though Pax had struck him.

"He is injured again?" Pax asked.

Draven ground his teeth together. "Not that he'll admit," he grated.

"But—?" Pax prompted.

"He's moving wrong. Worse than usual, I mean." Draven's jaw worked. "And he... he fucking *puked his guts out* right after he took the courier through the subspace barrier in the wormhole. Tried to pass it off as space sickness, but *come on.* Ash? Getting *space sick*?"

Pax agreed it was unlikely. Almost as out of character, in fact, as the idea of Ash failing to come up with a more believable cover story.

"He looked so pale and out of it for a minute afterward that I took over the controls and docked us myself," Draven continued. "Skye tried to get him to go to medical, but he waved it off and tried to act like he was fine. Said Ryder was busy and he wasn't gonna bother her with an upset stomach."

"Ryder *is* busy," Pax pointed out.

Draven scowled at him.

"But I will see to him instead," he finished.

The scowl grew deeper. "Good luck with that, unless you want to pick him up by the scruff of the neck and carry him to medical. I only came down here because I was getting dangerously tempted to try it myself. Fucker's probably got a blaster hidden on him somewhere, or I might've done."

"Brute force would not be my preferred method," Pax said, without explicitly ruling it out.

As though his excessive exertion had just caught up with him, Draven managed a half-controlled collapse into a seated position on the floor of the training room. A quick scan showed his body temperature and pulse already returning to acceptable levels, leading Pax to diagnose a non-hazardous combination of physical and emotional reaction.

"Prophets, Pax," he said, his eyes focused on nothing. "The eight of us... we're not going to make it out of this mess alive, are we?"

Quoting odds and variables didn't seem like a helpful response under the circumstances, so he merely said, "There is no way to predict the future with any accuracy. I will ensure that Ash's injuries are diagnosed and treated if necessary. Hunter is arranging a shift rota. Check in with him once you've cleaned up."

With a final scan to make sure Draven's pulse and breathing had returned to normal, Pax left him seated on the floor and went to find Ash.

TEN

As it happened, Ash was currently debating the merits of knocking back another shot of the whiskey Skye had liberated from the station's stores. On the negative side, doing so would mean moving from his position slumped over the table with his head resting on his arms. There were other very rational reasons why getting shit-faced right now would be a bad idea, probably. He wasn't entirely certain he cared. However, there were also very rational and compelling reasons why moving before he absolutely had to would be a bad idea.

"Ash," Temple said, "don't take this the wrong way, but you look like the aftermath of a radioactive freighter crash."

Ash grunted.

"Maybe you should listen to Skye and fucking *go to medical*, yeah?" he continued, not taking the subtly delivered hint.

Temple and Skye were seated across the table from him, forming the opposite points of a triangle anchored by one very battered and nauseated corner. Ash was torn between wishing they'd both go away, and being grateful that they'd dug up the booze and brought it here.

"I'm fine," he mumbled against the chipped duraplast surface of the table. "Long week, that's all."

The low noise of disapproval sounded like it came from Skye. He ignored it. When a large hand closed over his forearm, though, there was no ignoring the jolt of instinctive panic that had him lunging upright—or the blazing pain in his lower back as his muscles tightened unexpectedly. A sound he didn't recognize emerged from his throat as he jerked his arm free of Temple's light grip with a violent tug. His heart hammered against his chest, and he panted, trying to breathe through the irrational surge of panic.

Both Skye and Temple were looking at him with wide eyes; Temple's hands were raised in the universal gesture of '*shit, sorry man—this is me backing the fuck off.*'

"I believe we talked about you touching me when I'm not expecting it," Ash managed, once he was reasonably confident of his voice. The pounding of his pulse against his throat echoed the rhythm of the stabbing agony near his spine. "Though I guess now that I'm up, you can pour me another double."

Temple let his hands fall to the table, palms down. "*Ash*. Seriously. What. The. *Fuck.*"

Skye was glaring at him, worry warring with anger. "Tell him, Ash. Or I will."

He ignored the thinly veiled threat and reached—very, very carefully—for the bottle. The trick, he thought, would be drinking enough whisky to pass out, without throwing up again during the process and having to start over.

"Tell me what?" Temple asked, his dark brows furrowed over clear brown eyes.

Ryder had done well for herself with that one— he was a handsome man, Ash thought, bringing the shot glass to his lips now that his galloping heart had started to slow. The whiskey slid over his tongue, smooth and warm.

Skye was still scowling at him. "He's been trying to cozy up to some vicious Regime bastard by playing *seelaht*," she said tightly, "and if he's not careful, he's going to get himself killed, one way or another."

One way or another.

Oh, good. Apparently the alcohol was starting to work, because that actually struck him as rather funny.

He lowered the empty shot glass to the table. "I'm not a *seelaht*, Skye."

Temple was moving his eyes back and forth between them, like someone watching a hoverball match. "Whoa," he said. "Back up a minute. A *seelaht*? Like… the porn thing? With the collars and the…?" He trailed off, miming a gesture like someone cracking a whip.

Skye's scandalized gaze flew to him. "*Whoa!* Back up a minute, yourself! You… watch Vithii *porn*?"

To his credit, Temple didn't back down from his foster sister's flashing blue gaze. Ash took advantage of the momentary respite to pour another shot.

"Sorry, little sis, but I've watched a wide and eclectic selection of porn over the years," Temple was saying. "This was human porn, though. With actors playing the Vithii parts. You know how the Vithii are about anything to do with sex. But… maybe it would be better for our mental health if you didn't ask me any more questions about my porn viewing habits."

Skye blushed scarlet, and Temple returned his attention to Ash, narrowing his eyes. "So... as I was saying. Like the porn thing?" he pressed.

"I'm not a *seelaht*," Ash repeated, feeling like he was stuck in a looped recording.

By now, Skye had recovered enough from her adorable bout of moral outrage to focus on him again, like a terrier with a bone.

"Oh? What would you call it, then?" she demanded.

Ash glanced at the bottle of whisky, feeling like he should be drunker than he was. "A *seelaht* is female," he said absently. "A male is a *veelaht*, and the connotations are somewhat different because of the Vithii views regarding homosexuality."

Skye wasn't backing down. "Are you or are you not letting Regime perverts beat the shit out of you and rape you, in the hopes that they'll let slip sensitive information when they're flapping their lips in the afterglow?"

Ash let out a huff of something that might have been laughter, but wasn't. "That's not why I'm doing it. Though it is occasionally a useful side benefit."

He was too exhausted to parse the expression Temple was wearing, so he didn't try.

"Then why are you doing it?" Skye insisted.

The door to the canteen slid open, sending Ash's heart racing again. *Damn it.* He glared at the bottle of whiskey. Clearly, the fucking thing was defective.

Pax's raspy monotone came from the open doorway. "The bondmate of the Adjunct to the Premiere's Clandestine Operations office is a longtime friend of the human ambassador from the planet Terra Nova to the planet Vithara. Ash hopes to gain access to Ambassador Martinez via the Adjunct's household."

Ash toasted the cyborg with the empty shot glass. "What he said."

Hmm. That last part had come out a bit slurred. Also, the stabbing pain in his lower back felt a bit distant now, like something had wrapped it in a layer of fuzzy wool. Maybe the whiskey was redeeming itself after all.

"Fucking hell, Ash," Temple whispered.

"*It's not worth your life,*" Skye said, her voice sounding strained... and a bit like it was coming through a tunnel.

"Isn't it?" he asked.

"Certainly not today," Pax said. "You two, please leave us for a few moments. I brought a medical kit, and will treat any injuries that need to be treated."

A vague thread of worry penetrated Ash's growing haze of exhaustion and drunkenness, but he was distracted by Skye leaning down with both hands flat on the table, staring laser beams at him until he met her eyes blearily.

"Don't be a martyr for this cause, gods-damn it," she said with such intensity that he frowned. "*I never asked for martyrs.*"

Then, she pushed off the table and walked away. The door opened and closed, and Ash ran a shaky hand over his face, trying to decide if another drink would tip his stomach into full-blown rebellion. Movement registered in his peripheral vision, and a large, masculine hand moved the bottle out of reach.

A large, masculine, *Vithii* hand.

That hand closed on Ash's upper arm, and the switch inside his brain flipped, locking the air in his lungs as his vision tunneled in from the sides.

A male voice said, "Remove your shirt now. I will not accept refusal in this matter," and Ash's mind flew away.

Twenty minutes later, Pax stood in the corner of the medical bay as unobtrusively as a two-and-a-half meter tall cyborg could manage. He crossed his arms as he watched over both of Ryder's patients—splitting his attention between the brain monitor hooked into Veila'ana's readings and the interaction occurring on the other side of the room.

He'd seen enough cases of dissociation among organic soldiers on the battlefield to recognize it in a human. As soon as Ash's eyes went blank and distant, Pax had replayed their previous interaction and realized what must have happened. At which point, he'd propelled the now-pliant human up from his chair and dragged him straight to Ryder.

Ash could walk, albeit a bit unsteadily. He did not appear overtly panicked, and his vitals were normal except for a low-grade fever and accelerated breathing that—along with his recent medical history and Draven's mention of vomiting—made Pax suspect a kidney contusion or laceration.

When he'd chivvied Ash into the medical bay, Ryder had taken one look at him, cursed in a way that would have done a career soldier proud, and draped the human over a chair, arranging him to straddle the seat the wrong way so she could access his back. Then she'd run a scanner over his body, and cursed some more. Her eyes held the same look of helpless anger Skye's had held—the same anger Draven's had. Without looking at Pax directly, she jerked her chin toward Veila'ana and said, "Watch her."

So Pax watched the ambassador's readings with one eye, and Ash with the other, as Ryder set her scanner aside and crouched in front of the backward chair, just out of arm's reach.

Her tone changed to something completely different from its usual gruff growl as she quietly asked, "*Leetha*? It's Ryder. Can you answer me?"

She repeated the question every twenty seconds or so, until Ash blinked, winced in pain, and said, "Ryder? Where—" His hoarse voice broke off, and he swallowed. "Why... am I in the medbay?" Then he stirred as if to rise, only to freeze, the muscles in his back going rigid.

"Three guesses?" Ryder said, her earlier softness disappearing in favor of her usual sarcasm.

"Shit," Ash breathed.

"You have a two-centimeter contusion on your left kidney, with minor internal bleeding," she began mercilessly. "And apparently, you thought achieving a blood alcohol level of point-one-nine percent would somehow help with that problem."

"I checked out on Pax, didn't I," Ash said quietly. It wasn't a question.

"Yes," Ryder said without hesitation. "He's here, by the way—watching Veila'ana's readings for me while I deal with your scrawny, self-destructive human ass. Now, take your damned shirt off, or I'll take a protoplaser to it and do it myself."

There was a faintly awkward pause, and Ash said, "You'll have to use the protoplaser, Doc. I don't think I can lift my left arm above shoulder height right now without passing out."

"You're an idiot, *leetha*," Ryder said, and retrieved the instrument. She cut his shirt off with a few deft slices.

The bruising on the left half of the human's lower back was impressive. The darkest area also looked remarkably like a boot print. Ryder did not comment, but Pax imagined he could sense her gritting her teeth.

"It wasn't this bad earlier," Ash said in a soft tone. "I was going to find someone in the Capital to check for kidney damage, but then I got Kade's and Hunter's messages. It sounded time-sensitive, so I figured I'd have a quiet word with you once the patient who really needs your help was stable."

"Shall I just make a recording of me saying 'you're an idiot,' so I can play it every couple of minutes?" Ryder replied pointedly. "That would free me up to concentrate on preventing a retroperitoneal hemorrhage."

Ash paused for a beat. "Tell you what. I'll just shut up now. That's probably easier."

"Yes. It probably is."

Ryder rummaged through the medical equipment stores and came out with several items. Pax recognized a surgical drainage tube and a cutaneous anti-inflammatory waveform emitter.

"Want me to put you under first?" Ryder asked.

Ash shook his head. "No. A local's fine." His voice was tired. "You never know when the next crisis will pile on."

Ryder got to work, and before a quarter cycle had passed, Ash was listing to one side, clearly on the verge of sleep. She steadied him and glanced at Pax.

"Have someone drag a spare cot in here, before he face-plants on the damned deck plates."

Pax made the call, and Skye and Temple arrived with the requested item in short order.

"Need anything else, Red?" Temple asked, once Ash was settled on his front on the thin mattress, dead to the world, the waveform emitter secured over his left kidney.

Ryder spared Temple a wan half-smile. "Another medic and a couple of orderlies?" she suggested.

Skye crossed her arms, holding them tight to her body. "He'll be all right, though?" she asked.

"I imagine he'll have a headache like an unstable quasar when he wakes up," Ryder said. "Though I don't expect it to teach him anything. The kidney should be all right. And if it's not?" She shrugged. "He's got a spare."

Temple shook his head at her. "Medical humor. Never understood it."

She raised an eyebrow. "When the alternative is throwing things against the wall, you learn to appreciate it," she said dryly. "Now, out—both of you. I'm busy."

Temple huffed and planted a human-style kiss on Ryder's forehead. Pax saw her lean into it almost imperceptibly. When the two humans left after Skye shot a final long, unhappy look at Ash, Pax caught Ryder's eye.

"The ambassador's readings are showing a ninety percent reversal in brain infiltration," he reported.

Ryder's expression lightened, and she crossed to see the readouts for herself. "So they do. That's quicker than I expected, to be honest. I want at least a ninety-nine-point-five percent reversal before I start excising the implant. But at this rate, that may be within the next cycle or two."

"I will stay and assist you," Pax said, not wanting to risk her attention being split between two patients during such a delicate procedure.

"Thanks," she said, sparing him a tired smile. "In the mean time, why don't you draft an updated report for Hunter, while I take some fresh samples of the bot population inside that implant?"

Pax nodded agreeably, and turned to his assigned task.

ELEVEN

By station evening, Ash had been sent to sleep off the rest of his headache in a private room, while Ambassador Veila'ana recovered from surgery, still under sedation. Ryder was cautiously optimistic that the implant had not caused lasting brain damage, but she wanted the swelling around the surgical site to go down before attempting to wake her patient.

Given Pax's description of Veila'ana's behavior the first time he'd tried to rouse her, Ryder was in no hurry to risk her delicate cranial repairs in the event of another violent reaction. Pax was also content to wait, especially since Ryder was in need of a few cycles' sleep herself by that point. Temple had come in earlier with food and drink, then waited rather pointedly while Ryder consumed it.

Now, Ryder was napping on the spare cot that Ash had recently vacated, while Pax watched over the ambassador.

She fascinated him, and not merely because she held possible answers to his very serious questions about what was happening inside the cyborg program. True—that was important, and by rights it should be his highest priority. But there were other mysteries surrounding Veila'ana, as well. Mysteries of a more... personal nature.

How could she possibly cause him to experience emotions, when the part of his brain that processed emotion had been gone for years? And would she still be able to do that after what the doctors and technicians on the orbital station had done to her? Did Pax even want her to try?

Such speculation was a waste of resources that could better be devoted to more practical pursuits. Her telepathic abilities would recover, or they would not. Ryder seemed optimistic about the surgery's success, but only time would tell.

Pax checked the readings as he had done every quarter cycle since Ryder started napping. This time, the inflammatory markers had finally dropped below the benchmark level she had specified, as the bone-knitting drugs and healing infrared waves completed their work. The place along Veila'ana's temple where the metal implant had been was raised with fresh scar tissue, the skin silvery. No doubt a cosmetic surgeon could erase the visual evidence completely, but Ryder had been more concerned with efficiency than aesthetics given their current tenuous circumstances.

He rose and crossed to the second cot, closing his hand over Ryder's shoulder. He could have simply called out to her—she was a light sleeper after nearly half a lifetime in the medical profession. But waking her was a reasonable excuse to touch her, something all of them except Kade had made a point of doing more often since learning of her misguided reasons for avoiding contact with them. Not that Kade was offended by Ryder's *grei'kaapt* status, of course; he was similarly standoffish with all of them.

Ryder jerked awake, blinking into focus and swinging her legs off the bed on autopilot. "Problem?" she rasped.

"No," Pax told her. "The ambassador's markers have dropped below the levels you specified. If it is safe, we need her awake as soon as possible."

Ryder ran a hand over her face and nodded. "Oh. Okay. That's good. Let me look over the most recent scan and I'll make a determination." A huge yawn cracked her jaw, and she stretched, joints popping.

Pax waited with a machine's patience as Ryder confirmed that Veila'ana was sufficiently recovered from the nanotech reversal and cranial surgery to be brought out of her induced coma.

"She's ready," Ryder said.

"Do you wish me to inform the others?" Pax asked, but she only shook her head.

"No. I don't want a crowd underfoot. In fact, don't allow her skin-to-skin contact with either of us until we know exactly what we're dealing with here," she instructed. "Given what you've told me, there's a chance her abilities could be out of control. She might do damage to one of us even if she didn't intend to."

It was an aspect he hadn't considered. He frowned then, because he *should* have considered it. How strange that he hadn't.

"Very well," he said absently, and retrieved the blanket from the cot Ryder had vacated. He placed it over Veila'ana's body without touching her directly, tucking it up to her chin, so that all of her bare skin below the neck was safely covered. Meanwhile, Ryder donned gloves.

"I'm turning on the stasis field first, just in case," Ryder informed him, and flipped the switch that would keep her patient encased in a forcefield until they could determine Veila'ana's mental state.

Then, she retrieved the hypo-injector that would wake the ambassador from her induced coma, and emptied its contents into the vein under her jaw. As before, there was no response at first.

"Ambassador Veila'ana," Ryder said very slowly and clearly. "It's Ryder, from the prison. Pax is here as well. You've been unconscious, but I've healed your injuries as much as I can, and you're going to be fine. You're in a stasis field so you don't accidentally hurt yourself while you're getting your bearings. Please stay calm; I'll release it as soon as you're properly awake. Now. Can you hear me?"

Pax focused closely on Veila'ana's face, and was rewarded by a small twitch as her eyebrows drew together.

Nahleene frowned, a low moan slipping free of her throat. Her face felt oddly numb, except for a strange pulling sensation at her left temple. Words trickled into her awareness, along with a confusing tangle of sensory perception—cool air against a stinging spot on the side of her throat... a soft, heavy weight draped over her body... a sense of confinement around her limbs. Her head ached abominably with a dull, pounding throb. There were people nearby, minds humming around her, but it was all muddled together, jarring her senses.

She scrunched her eyes shut, and the next sound that jerked free from her throat was more a grunt of displeasure than anything else. Belatedly, the sense of the words she'd heard earlier started to sink in. *Unconscious. Stasis field. Ryder and... Pax?*

She'd been dreaming.

Maybe.

At least, she had vague memories of something nightmarish. Memories of terrifying *things*, walking and talking creatures that looked like Vithii, but with no living minds behind their eyes. Memories of being alone, but surrounded by ghosts. Solid ghosts; beings that she could touch with her hands, but not with her mind. Her eyes flew open, her limbs jerking with the instinctive need to move— only to be brought up short by that unseen constraint around her body.

"That's the stasis field. Please stay calm." She recognized Ryder's voice more easily this time, and tried to match it with one of the dancing, whirling mental presences spinning just beyond her reach.

"Where?" she croaked.

A different voice spoke. *Pax.* "We are in an abandoned lunar outpost situated near the outer boundaries of the Ilarian system. We are secure, for the moment."

Now that she focused on it more carefully, she thought one of the chaotic presences jangling along her nerves might be a cyborg. A *normal* cyborg, though. Not like... not... like...

Oh, *shit*.

Memory started to filter in, and her pulse rate increased. "Let me up," she said, a bit desperately. Practicality raised a cautious head, and she added, "But don't touch me. Something feels... wrong with my telepathy."

The blanket was too warm where it lay across her body—the stasis field too confining, and she needed to *move*.

"We won't touch you." Ryder's voice, no-nonsense and dispassionate. "Stay calm, Ambassador. I'm releasing the field now, but you may experience weakness or dizziness if you try to get up too soon."

Nahleene gritted her teeth, just needing the damned forcefield off. It buzzed, the invisible weight across her body falling away. She took in rapid breaths, trying to dispel the feeling of suffocation. A hand fell on her upper arm through the blanket. The mind behind it was muffled by the heavy fabric, but very much present. She blinked the last of the blurriness from her eyes and looked up to find Pax standing over her, his expression impassive as he watched her face closely.

She swallowed against the dryness in her throat. "I was… on the orbital platform where they do R&D for the cyborg program," she said slowly. "There was… something…"

She shook her head, trying to dislodge more memories. "They caught me spying and arrested me. But… the cyborgs there. They…" She swallowed again. "What did they do to me? How did I get here?"

She very cautiously inched herself into a sitting position, Pax's loose grip falling away as she did. Lifting a hand free of the blanket, she raised it to her aching head, feeling the raised lines of fresh scars beneath her fingertips. *Argh.* Her brain felt like someone had tried to make an omelet with it…

What the fuck had they *done* to her?

Pax was still hovering, if a giant, tough-looking cyborg soldier could be said to hover. It was he who answered.

"I am unable to relate any firsthand details, but Kade and I were monitoring the orbital platform's transmissions, as we agreed ahead of time. The station commander requested information on your security clearance from the Capital, along with guidance on whether or not to detain you. A return transmission ordered him to take both you and Jodor Erisuel into custody, and to ship you back to Ilarius."

A sharp, indrawn breath drew Nahleene's attention to Ryder, who was staring at Pax with a gaze like twin laser beams. Pax lifted his eyes and returned the look evenly.

"I did not tell you sooner about your bondmate's presence because I did not want you emotionally compromised during a delicate medical procedure," he said.

As whacked as Nahleene's thought processes were right now, she couldn't help wincing on Ryder's behalf. *Ouch.* For her part, Ryder went very still and very cold, but merely said, "We'll discuss this later. Only... tell me now. Is he alive or dead?"

"He is dead. I made certain of it." Pax returned his gaze to Nahleene. "Kade and I intercepted the transport you were on and disabled it so we could retrieve you. Then we brought you here."

Nahleene was still looking at Ryder, who had gone pale—all the blood drained from her face.

"You're sure Jodor didn't make it out?" the medic asked.

"Completely," Pax said.

Ryder felt behind her for a chair and sat in it, rather abruptly. Pax frowned, as though realizing belatedly that he could have handled the verbal exchange with a bit more tact. Nahleene raised a hand to her aching head again, wishing that her brain cells would work properly. Maybe it was selfish under the circumstances, but...

"You still haven't told me what they did to me. Either of you. Something's wrong. In my head. Tell me what they *did*."

Ryder jerked herself free of her shocked state with a deep breath. "Right. Sorry. As far as we can determine, the doctors and technicians on the platform interfered with the telepathic centers of your brain by implanting a cranial device. It used bots to scramble your synapses. I reversed the infiltration using different bots taken from Pax's blood, and surgically removed the implant once the original nanotech was destroyed."

Nahleene's heart thudded against her chest as fresh memories of waking, but being unable to sense anything around her trickled in. "Shit. *Shit.*" It had been like losing a limb. Like losing her hearing or eyesight. And while that horrifying sensation of being mind-blind was gone, in its place, everything was now a confused swirl. She was desperate to reach out, to find some way to anchor herself mentally, but she didn't dare. Gods knew what her touch would do to a non-telepath when she was in this state.

"Have your telepathic senses returned?" Pax asked.

She opened and closed her mouth a couple of times before the words came out. "S-sort of. It's all out of kilter. I... need..." Nahleene shook her head, trying to clear it, and regretted it immediately. The pain went some way toward focusing her thoughts, though, and she changed tack. "It doesn't matter now. I have to tell you what I saw, before I was detained."

"You were able to observe the program?" Pax asked, sounding almost eager.

"Yeah," she said, still kneading her forehead as if it would somehow hold back the headache caused by having nanotech burrowing into her brain. And gods. *Fuck*. She could *not* let herself think about that too closely or she was really going to lose it. Instead, she focused on reporting what she'd learned... as if that wasn't upsetting enough. "Yeah, I got an eyeful, all right. Some clever, twisted bastard in R&D realized that if you're going to use nanotech to enhance a Vithii body, there's no particular reason you need to start with someone who's alive."

There was a beat of absolute silence. If Ryder had been pale before, her complexion now was the color of chalk.

Unsurprisingly, Pax recovered first. "When I boarded the transport to retrieve you, one of the guards was a cyborg. A new kind of cyborg. The discrepancy was difficult to quantify, but there was... no indication of a living mind behind the technology."

"It was a reanimated corpse," Nahleene said, feeling nausea join the headache. "One driven only by nanotech and an AI."

Pax was silent again, but then his head moved back and forth in a slow, negative shake.

"That... does not seem feasible. Artificial intelligence is useful in many applications, but it is not sufficiently advanced to control every aspect of a cyborg's physical and mental existence," he said.

"The guard I fought reacted in too complex a manner."

Nahleene closed her eyes, but that just worsened the sense of everything spinning around her, out of control.

"It's not that simple, Pax," she said. "The AI. It's not just lines of code. Jodor said they've been downloading the minds of cyborgs for years, right before they were decommissioned. They're controlling reanimated cyborgs with the combined memories and experiences of cyborgs that they've already killed."

Pax blinked, processing the ambassador's words. In an instant, several puzzle pieces slotted into place. Before he could open his mouth to say anything, however, he was cut off by the sound of Ryder's chair screeching across the deck plates as she shot to her feet. He looked at her, realizing that his distraction had kept him from noting how much the emotional impact of the last few minutes had affected her.

Unacceptable.

"Ryder," he began.

She was breathing in hard, controlled bursts, though, and she shook her head sharply. "No. Pax... Ambassador... I can't have this conversation right now. I need a cycle or two."

Pax did a quick mental rundown of the current situation—Veila'ana's physical condition, Ash's physical condition, the general security of the outpost, and what he now understood about the developments in the cyborg program. There was time for Ryder to deal with her psychological reaction to learning of her estranged bondmate's death, followed closely by information about the decommissioned cyborgs that she obviously found upsetting. Her absence for a couple of cycles would not endanger anyone.

He nodded. "I apologize, Ryder. I misjudged the effects that the revelations of the past few minutes would have on an emotional being. Please, go find Temple and do whatever is necessary to begin processing this information in a healthy way."

She stared at him. "*'Processing this information in a healthy way'*? Fucking hell. Sometimes it's like you don't even know me at all."

He held her gaze. "Find Temple. Give me your word, Ryder. I will stay here, and inform you if you are needed for any emergencies."

"Pax—"

"Your word, Ryder, or I'll call Temple myself and have him come here to get you," he said, inexorable. "You are not alone. You were never alone. So please do not continue to act as though you are. And accept my apologies for failing to adequately take your emotions into account."

Ryder clenched her jaw for a moment... and then slumped. "I'll go find him. Just tell me first—Jodor. Did you kill him yourself?"

"Yes," Pax said without hesitation. "A point-blank blaster shot through the heart. It was quick."

She wrapped her arms around herself and nodded, her eyes unfocused. Pax checked his system connection with the station's internal sensors, locating the two human males and quickly pinpointing the one not in the quarters where Ash was sleeping.

"Temple is in the fitness room. He is currently alone. Go."

She nodded again, her gaze still distant. "Just… for a cycle or two. Then I'll help you figure out what to do about… all this." She focused on him, anguish in her brown eyes. "Gods, Pax. Sometimes I just get so tired. You know?"

He nodded, acknowledging the words and the weariness behind them. Even in her current state, Ryder took a few moments to check Veila'ana's medical readings before she left, giving Pax a final, troubled look as the door closed behind her. He followed her progress using the station sensors, ensuring that she did, in fact, go to the fitness room. The privacy lock engaged, and the readings for the two figures inside merged, Vithii and human melded so closely that they overlapped.

Veila'ana broke the silence.

"That was deftly handled, for someone who by rights shouldn't be able to feel or understand compassion." Her voice sounded strained.

Pax noted that the ambassador's pallor was not that much different than Ryder's had been. "You conflate feeling compassion with understanding compassion," he said. "Interesting."

Veila'ana looked taken aback. "I… well… yes. I suppose I do. Or did until today, at any rate."

"Ryder is my friend," Pax said. "I don't have so many of those that I can afford to hurt one of them, and not attempt to make amends afterward."

"You really did manipulate her like a pro, earlier, you know," she said. "Holding back the information about her bondmate being on that transport, so she wouldn't be upset when she was... doing whatever she did to get that implant out of me."

She shivered, as though a cold draft had blown across her skin.

"My revelation about the Under-Minister's presence and subsequent death was clumsy and ill-considered," Pax said. "I've become distracted by this mission."

Veila'ana rubbed at her forehead, as she had been doing intermittently since waking. "Count your blessings. I've apparently become brain-damaged by this mission. What's wrong with me? What did that implant do to me?"

He regarded her more closely. "The brain scans indicate that the removal of the implant and its associated nanotech was successful. The damage appears to have been reversed except for some very minor swelling around the surgical site. Perhaps the lingering effects are merely due to the extended period of sedation and unconsciousness. What symptoms are you experiencing?"

She dug her fingers harder into her forehead for a moment before deliberately lowering her hand. Her expression was pained.

"It's hard to explain to a non-telepath. When I woke up before, I was mind-blind. It was like waking up blind and deaf, and I panicked. Now, I can sense minds again, but everything's off-kilter. It's like this big, confusing swirl. Like standing in pitch darkness in a field, surrounded by glowbugs, only you have vertigo and the lights are spinning around you instead of staying still."

"Are you in pain?" Pax asked, aware that he should have checked before sending Ryder away. "Nauseated?"

Veila'ana sighed. "Yes and yes. It's tolerable, but what's worse is the growing compulsion to link minds with someone, when there's no one here to do it with."

Pax frowned. "I do not understand."

She gestured vaguely. "When a Maelfian undergoes any kind of telepathic trauma, part of the treatment is usually to link minds with a mind healer—or sometimes with a close family member or mate, if no healer is available. Maelfians can redirect mental energy into healing energy, but when the mind is the thing that's injured, it needs outside help before the process can work."

Pax realized that the only specific medical information he knew about the Maelfian species was that which related to killing them efficiently on the battlefield.

"I was unaware," he said.

She shrugged. "It's also a way of reorienting the psychic senses, and grounding them. I'm no healer, but I'd guess that's probably what I need. Although it's kind of a moot point out here in the back of beyond."

Pax thought of the sharp, shocking sensations that followed linking with her back on Ilarius, and his own ambivalent reaction to feeling the emotion she thrust at him.

"Could you not draw mental energy for healing from a psi-null individual?" he asked.

Veila'ana's eyes flew to his. "A psi-null?" she echoed. "I... don't know. But I do know trying might be dangerous. My telepathic senses are scrambled. It could be intensely traumatic to an unshielded mind with no psychic defenses."

After weighing the potential outcomes, Pax made a decision.

"Then it is as well you have access to an individual who is incapable of experiencing emotional trauma, and highly resistant to physical trauma."

She looked at him as though he'd gone mad. "Pax... do I need to remind you that I put you on your ass in the back room of that club without even intending to?"

But he saw her hands twitch, as though she had to stop herself from reaching for him. She clenched them into fists by her sides.

He shrugged. "That is easily remedied. I will sit down this time before you make the attempt."

That startled a bark of laughter from her, and she flinched as the sudden outburst apparently pained her.

"Ow. *Damn it*." She lifted a hand to her head again. "Seriously, though—this is ridiculous. Do you even understand what you're agreeing to?"

"A psychic connection for the purpose of reorienting your telepathic senses and funneling mental energy to physical healing. Veila'ana," he said, only to stop and correct himself. "Nahleene, *you* must understand that I have already had outsiders make extensive alterations to my brain—up to and including the removal of my free will. Until our first encounter in the Capital, those alterations also included the destruction of my ability to experience emotion. I am—" Pax paused, searching for the appropriate words. "I am willing to risk the prospect of encountering negative emotions for a short time, if it would be helpful to your recovery. Because that is still more than I ever thought to experience again."

The ambassador—*Nahleene*—gave him such a look of combined doubt and longing that he thought at first she would refuse. But eventually, her expression cleared, and she took a centering breath.

"Okay," she said. "Here's what we're going to do." She took a corner of the heavy blanket and wrapped it around her left forearm. "Get that chair over here and sit down. Then hold my wrist, but don't let our skin touch. I'll touch the side of your face, and if it's too much, you can pull my hand away. That will break the contact instantly."

"Logical," he said, and went to retrieve the chair.

When he was settled, she gave him another searching look. "Shouldn't you... I don't know... check with Ryder about this first?"

He raised an eyebrow. "That would be counterproductive, since she would immediately forbid the attempt. Am I correct that there is no danger to you in the joining?"

She shook her head. "No. This might or might not help me, but it won't hurt me. You're the one taking the risk."

"If I am in distress, I will remove your hand as you have instructed," he said simply, and grasped her wrist in a careful grip through the cloth wrapped around it.

Her gaze was piercing, but then she tilted her head, birdlike. "Guess you really are a rebel, huh?" she asked.

"In more ways than one," he agreed.

A smile quirked her lips, but then she sobered. "Last chance to rethink this plan," she said softly.

When he didn't react, she lifted warm fingers to rest on the unblemished side of his face.

He closed his eyes, focusing inward.

Receipt

Pork Banh Mi x 1	£7.00
↳ 1 x No spicy - £0.00	
Tofu Garlic Noodle x 1	£8.00
Steak Garlic Noodle x 1	£9.00
↳ 1 x Well done - £0.00	
Steak Garlic Noodle x 1	£9.00
↳ 1 x Medium - £0.00	
Vegan Feast x 1	£9.00
↳ 1 x Rice - £0.00	
Bun Bo Nuong x 1	£8.50
Bun Cha Hanoi x 1	£8.00

	Vat	£9.75
	Total	**£58.50**

Sumup:	£58.50
Change due:	£0.00

Card Payment	£58.50
VISA	**** **** **** 9139
Auth Code:TDK7SHZRKT	
Reference:TDK7SHZRKT	

VAT NO: 390050620

Thank You!

28th Feb 12:52 PM 1646052752513

TWELVE

Nahleene tried to ignore the small, internal voice whispering that this was a foolish idea. That voice was buried under the much louder part of her brain that was clamoring for contact—something to anchor her and drive away the awful feeling of isolation and mental confusion. Maelfians weren't meant to go for long periods without telepathic joining, and while she might have been half-Vitharan, she still felt that sense of distance; that awareness of being cut off from others and the world around her.

She had a sinking feeling that her judgment wasn't all it could be right now.

Pax's large hand gripped her arm lightly, and she knew her wrist would snap like a twig if the mental shock of their connection made him lose physical control for even an instant. Honestly, it made her feel a bit better, twisted though the sentiment probably was. She was asking him to risk psychic trauma, but at least she was risking crushed bones in return. It was additional motivation to keep her mental shit together, right? And it's not like Ryder couldn't put her wrist back together afterward, if worse came to worst.

Yep, it looked like her brain was really pulling out the stops when it came to justifying this risk. Damn it... she just needed the world to stop spinning so she could think straight. Pax was a battle-hardened cyborg, and all he had to do was move her hand a fraction away from his face if he needed her to stop. That was perfectly reasonable. Wasn't it?

Her fingers brushed his cool skin, and his eyes slipped closed as she sank into him.

Oh. *Oh*. Yes, this was so much better. Pax wasn't spinning like a leaf caught in the wind. He was centered. Immovable. She groaned in relief and burrowed deeper, needing more of this feeling of being grounded. His mind was so carefully ordered. She'd forgotten the feel of him—different from any other mind she'd ever touched.

She should be concentrating her efforts on not overwhelming him. That was important. But it was also hard, when she needed more, more, *more*—

More of the closeness. More of the sensation of another mind surrounding hers, thoughts twining together. She twirled around, trying to take everything in at once. As before, the part of his mind that was accessible to her was grounded completely in the present. She could only see the parts of him that he actively called to the forefront. There were no currents of emotion to ride... no rivers of reminiscence or waterfalls of speculation to navigate.

I am willing to risk the prospect of encountering negative emotions for a short time, because that is still more than I ever thought to experience again, he'd said.

Nahleene couldn't help the wash of sadness as she remembered his words, and the reason behind them. Sadness on his behalf... anger towards the people who had done this to him... disgust over the new and terrible things those same people were willing to do to the dead, using the minds of the murdered.

Pax's hand tightened on her wrist, but not to the point of pain. Still, it was enough to recall a small corner of her awareness to the present, and to make her realize that she was doing exactly what he'd been resigned to—flooding him with negative emotion. She drew up short, wrestling her mind under firmer control. She could do better than this. He *deserved* better than this.

Consciously, she considered what she'd seen of him so far. How many people, after being violated in the way he had been, would dedicate their lives to fighting injustice? How many would seek friendship instead of revenge, and cultivate the emotional health of those around them even though they could no longer feel emotion? Seeing him do all of those things engendered a tangle of feelings that included both respect and more than a hint of awe. Thinking about the way he'd risked his life to board a hostile spacecraft for the sole purpose of saving her from capture by the Ilarian Regime added gratitude to the list.

He inhaled sharply, his grip tightening incrementally around her arm before relaxing. Her fingertips picked up a fine tremor in the muscles of his face, which quickly stilled. All at once, she became aware of a sense of him sensing her—a feedback loop of the sort that was inevitable during contact between a telepath and a non-telepath.

Normally, the telepath could control such a loop, but Nahleene's shields were practically nonexistent right now—part of the damage caused by the assault on her brain. And right now, it wasn't helping that she didn't *want* to shut down that loop.

Through it, the connection grew deeper, Pax's thoughts and memories opening to her as his mind rode the borrowed currents of emotion.

His mental energy flowed together with hers, and her mind instinctively grasped at it, pulling it inside her to bolster her own reserves as her Maelfian healing abilities stirred. Scenes from his past started to wash into her awareness on the roiling tide, thrown up randomly as he struggled to put the emotion she was feeding him into context.

Even as the pain in her head subsided by gradual degrees, she relived the moment he'd received notification of his enlistment into a highly competitive top-secret program. She experienced his moment of horror upon realizing what that program truly was—the last emotion he'd experienced before the capacity to feel anything was surgically removed from him.

She felt him strive to come to terms with his reality upon unexpectedly regaining his free will while still within the cyborg program. Watched through his eyes as his batch siblings were vaporized, one by one, until only he was left. She felt him coldly weighing his options, before deciding on escape. Experienced his struggle to replace mindless compliance with some sort of existential framework in the absence of emotion or purpose.

He had drawn on memories of the man he'd been before he was changed, combined them with memories of others he'd respected, and somehow come up with an acceptable pattern for behavior when everything rational insisted he should have become a monster. And then, he'd stumbled upon others following the same sort of framework as the one he'd built from dust and recollection.

Justice for the oppressed. Freedom from fear. A world that gave the downtrodden a hand up instead of crushing them further into the dirt.

Gods above, she thought dazedly, aware on some distant level that she was weeping now, tears tracking down her cheeks.

She *had* to get closer to him—it was like a compulsion. As her mind funneled his borrowed strength into fixing synaptic connections and healing psychic damage, she was able to open herself to him further, letting him feel her emotions more deeply. More fully. In turn, more of his essence flowed into her—his past, his present, and his aspirations for the future.

The boundaries between them blurred, and the part of her that should have been shouting a warning fell beneath a landslide of need—the need to become one... to merge with him until nothing else existed except the connection binding them together.

At some point, he'd used his grip on her to pull her closer, and she'd apparently taken that as an excuse to slide off the cot and onto his lap, straddling him. It was even better this way—both of them angling to get more skin against skin. The blanket slid to the deck, forgotten. Gods, he was *strong*, hard muscles like steel cords flexing under her where her legs straddled his. She was wearing some kind of lightweight medical gown that crinkled like paper, tied closed at the front with a simple belt.

Distantly, she felt a jolt as her sex ground against his thigh, her nipples hardening as she pressed against the bulging muscles of his chest. Again, the compulsion swelled for *closer, deeper, more*, taking on a new and unexpected dimension. Sexual desire flooded the mental connection, ricocheting back and forth like a laser beam inside a hall of mirrors. Somehow, her lips had ended up pressed to the juncture of his neck and shoulder.

With no thought beyond the need reflecting between them in ever tightening waves, she bared her teeth and bit down hard. She was rewarded an instant later with the twitch of hardening flesh against the crease of her inner thigh, at the same time she experienced his emotional blowback from her growing lust. Her left hand was still clamped to the side of his face, but her right hand scrabbled between them for the fastenings of his trousers, pulling and tugging until his cock slipped free, pulsing in her hand.

———◆———

Pax let his head fall back, baring his neck to Nahleene's teeth as feelings he had never thought to experience again rolled through his body and mind. A low groan escaped him, blood rushing to his cock, making him harden spontaneously for the first time in more than a dozen years.

Cyborgs could still achieve reflex erections—nothing physically prevented them from growing hard and ejaculating under direct stimulation, although they were sterile. However, they did not get psychogenic erections resulting from sexual thoughts or desires, and they did not experience physical pleasure from stimulation or climax. For that reason, at least among Pax and his batch siblings, there had been no real impetus to engage in sexual behavior.

So, to say that his reaction to Nahleene's bite was unexpected was putting it mildly. Yet... perhaps it should not have been. At first, Pax had once again felt negative emotions flowing through the telepathic connection between them. Anger, disgust, grief. He'd let them come, focusing on the intriguing experience of feeling anything at all. Trying not to recoil or otherwise disrupt the link that Nahleene needed to recover from the damage to her psyche.

Then, the nature of the exchange had shifted. The connection grew deeper; the emotions grew softer. Positive emotions. Respect and gratitude—even affection. He latched onto them, unable to help himself, greedily attempting to identify the nuances even as he pulled them inside himself. It was overwhelming, yet he did not want it to stop. He wanted... *more*.

Twice, he had to stop himself from tightening his grip around Nahleene's delicate wrist, his fingers twitching. But he was unable to stop himself from reaching for her with his free arm, pulling her body closer in hopes that doing so would pull her mind closer as well. She let him. In fact, she seemed to be trying to do the same thing, crawling into his lap and straddling him in a way that was different—and so much better—than having her unconscious form curled against his while inside Kade's fighter.

She was naked under the flimsy paper gown Ryder had dressed her in for surgery, and her sex rubbed against his left thigh as she shifted in his grip. The friction sparked feelings inside her that transmitted straight to him—straight to a part of his mind that shouldn't have been able to process them. His eyes flew open, and he shuddered. When she bit him, the years fell away and he was once more a normal Vithii male holding a beautiful female in his arms, the desire to bed her flooding him as his erection stiffened and twitched.

He was distantly aware that there were probably other considerations that should be taken into account before proceeding further, but somehow they did not seem terribly pressing as Nahleene's free hand fumbled at the fastenings of his trousers and drew his length free. His flesh twitched and curled in her hand, *seeking*. Slickness dribbled from the head as her fingers squeezed around him and pumped—once... twice.

Her teeth were still buried in his neck as she shifted in his lap and guided him to her opening, lowering herself onto him. Her moan vibrated against the abused flesh where she was biting him. The pleasure she experienced as his cock stretched her passage flowed through the bond to him, melding seamlessly with the reflexive physical reaction of his nerve endings being stimulated.

He gasped, and bucked up. His hands closed around her hips, tight enough to leave bruises, and he felt her reaction to that, as well. Nahleene ripped her mouth away from his throat and echoed his gasp, the sound trailing into a low growl... almost a purr of satisfaction.

Pax lifted her hips and let her slide back down his length, needing to feel that pulse of pleasure again.

And again.

And *again*—over and over, growing deeper and more intense with every stroke. Her mind coiled around his, breaking into smaller and smaller fractals that wormed ever more inextricably into his thoughts. Her fingers still pressed against his cheek and forehead, though he had long since released his grip on her wrist. Her other hand found the hem of his black, utilitarian t-shirt and burrowed underneath, sliding over the flex of his abdominal muscles to splay across his heart.

Her growing desperation for both release and oneness transmitted itself to him, their movements together growing frenzied and sloppy as her climax approached. It broke over him like a wave, turning everything brilliant and staticky. He had a vague awareness of his muscles clenching and jerking as he pulsed inside her warm depths. She shuddered in his arms, while inside his mind a low hum of white noise blanketed him with the feeling of ever-expanding, boneless afterglow.

His knot swelled and the entrance to her passage clamped around it, locking them together. Her body draped over him, growing heavy and lax in his embrace.

"*Nahleene*," he breathed, feeling the absolute serenity of her coital trance settling over him like a comforting cloak. "What have you done to me?"

THIRTEEN

Nahleene knew on some deep level that she should worry more about what had just happened, but it was hard to worry about much of anything while emerging from the warm, lazy depths of a coital trance. Her passage fluttered around Pax's knot as it softened, sending a last few tendrils of shivery heat along her nerve endings.

His arms around her were strong. Reassuring. He'd been strangely quiet for a Vithii male during sex—usually, they couldn't shut up, murmuring an unedited stream-of-consciousness babble about anything and everything. Her mind was slowly uncurling from his as their bodies prepared to disengage, and she realized that his silence was probably due to the unusual way in which he'd experienced their union. With their thoughts and feelings twined so closely, he'd been as much a party to the coital trance as she had.

That must have been odd for him, as a male.

She'd slept with Vitharans before, back on the homeworld, but never when her telepathic shields were completely down like this. She'd also slept with a couple of Maelfians over the years, but it was a totally different experience when both parties were telepaths and could control the degree of mental overlap.

In fact, Nahleene didn't think she'd ever linked so completely to another person in her life. It had been… an experience, to put it mildly. But now, it was nearly over, and she had no idea what the repercussions were likely to be. She gradually reassembled her shields, being careful to use a gentle touch as she extricated herself from Pax's mind. His cheek rested against her hair; she could feel the fine filigree of his facial implants against her scalp. He shifted beneath her, a small noise of discontent slipping free from his lips.

That tiny sound pricked at her soul. She was withdrawing her emotions from him after sharing them like a banquet, leaving him once again without the ability to feel. A lump rose in her throat.

"Pax," she said, the word a hoarse rasp.

He lifted his head, and she eased back until she could meet his eyes. His blue-steel gaze was stormier than she remembered—a sea tossed by waves. As she watched, it grew flatter and more distant, the borrowed emotion behind it draining away as the last of her telepathic presence withdrew from him.

"I'm sorry," she whispered, shifting her hips until his softening length slipped free of her body, leaving her feeling as empty as he looked.

He blinked. "Was the mental connection unhelpful?"

The lump in her throat grew worse, and she swallowed to force it down.

"No," she said, voice still raspy. "No, it worked… very well."

His brows twitched. "Then why are you sorry?"

Strong, cool hands still rested over her hips, spanning them. She was suddenly very aware of the touch, even through the cheap, papery fabric of the ridiculous medical gown.

She swallowed again. "What I did to you just now was unethical. *Very* unethical. Sex with someone who was telepathically compromised and unable to give consent? I—"

Heat flooded her cheeks as the full import really started to hit her.

Pax still looked quizzical. "I am unable to either pass or receive sexually transmitted diseases. I am also sterile, so pregnancy is not a concern. I was able to feel through the mental connection that you were not hurt or distressed by the act. I do not understand the issue."

Nahleene opened and closed her mouth a couple of times before trying again. "I didn't get your consent first, Pax. I didn't even try, but if I had you still might not have been able to give it meaningfully. That's... kind of a big deal."

His expression smoothed. "Nahleene. This was the first time I have experienced the sensation of pleasure in twelve years, four months, and twenty-one days. We have already established that neither of us was harmed by the union. I still fail to understand your concern." His right eyebrow flickered up. "Though if you had paused to seek my explicit consent first, it might have made me stop and assess the situation long enough to engage the door's privacy lock before continuing."

Her mouth dropped open, a bubble of choked laughter lodging in her chest.

"Was that... a *joke*?" she asked, incredulous.

He lifted her back to sit on the edge of the medical cot as though she weighed nothing.

"An observation," he corrected, tucking himself away and re-fastening his trousers without any apparent concern. "Why? Was it amusing?"

"Yeah," she said, following his lead and wrapping the gown around herself properly. There was a small rip under the left arm. "It really was."

Her eyes strayed to the side of his neck, where she had a vague memory of biting the hell out of him. The mark was already healed, bots having swarmed to the site of the small injury to repair it.

"The station sensors show that Ryder is returning," Pax said evenly. "She will be here in a few moments."

Nahleene nodded. "Yes. I can feel her."

"Is that an indication you are mentally recovered?"

His words drew her focus back to his face and she dragged in a deep breath.

"Telepathically? I'm feeling much more myself, yes. The world isn't spinning, and I'm afraid I must have leeched more than enough energy from you to heal the broken connections. The pain is gone, too."

"Then it was energy well-spent," Pax said. "It is easily replaced, for me."

Nahleene shifted, suddenly all too aware of the damp feeling between her legs as Pax's release seeped from her passage. Of course, *that* was the signal for the unlocked medbay door to slide open, and Ryder to stride in with the air of someone on a mission. She was still pale, Nahleene noted, but she seemed to have regained the polished, prickly shell of detachment she normally wore like armor.

"Pax," she said, "I've been thinking about this concept of downloaded cyborg minds and what it might—"

The medic came to a halt so abrupt it was almost comical, staring at the two of them. Her nostrils flared, scenting the air, and Nahleene covered an embarrassed cringe. Ryder's eyes narrowed, focusing on Pax like a predator watching prey.

"You have got to be kidding me," she said. "Ninety minutes. I was gone for *ninety minutes!* Pax. What. The *actual. Fuck*?"

Clearly, Pax had been correct in his assumption that Ryder would have strong opinions regarding any unmonitored or experimental techniques applied to her patient in her absence. Though, in the medic's defense, even he could understand how the rather unmistakable smell of sex might be misinterpreted under the current circumstances. He opened his mouth to begin the explanation, but closed it again when Nahleene beat him to it.

"Don't bite Pax's head off, Ryder," she said, before Ryder could build up a full head of steam. "This was all me. In fact, I was just apologizing to him right before you came in."

"While I was attempting to explain that no apologies or self-recriminations were necessary," Pax added.

Ryder looked between the two of them, still with the air of someone who was one second away from blowing a gasket. "No," she said slowly and distinctly, "I'm pretty certain some recriminations *are* going to be necessary. I just need to figure out which direction to aim the cannons before I start firing. So maybe one or the other of you would like to stop babbling about apologies, and tell me what the ever-loving shit happened while I was gone?"

Nahleene forged ahead gamely. "My telepathic senses were impacted by the residual trauma from the implant you took out, as you know. Normally, the treatment for that kind of trauma in a Maelfian would involve mentally bonding with another person to kick-start psychic healing within the brain. Pax… uh…" She trailed off, looking at him uncertainly.

"I offered my services since I am generally resistant to physical and mental trauma," he said.

Nahleene nodded. "… And things got a bit out of hand when my body got confused between mental intimacy and physical intimacy," she finished. "Totally my fault, like I said."

Ryder continued to stare at them. After a pause long enough that an organic being would doubtless have found it uncomfortable, she scrubbed a hand over her face and sighed.

"Someday," she said, "I'd like to spend time around people who are sane and don't take imbecilic risks for no discernible reason. I think that would be very restful."

Her tone was oddly conversational and pleasant. Pax and Nahleene traded a look.

"Okay," Ryder went on. "You decided to try and drain psychic energy from a non-telepath to heal yourself. And you decided to do this without any medical personnel present to monitor the process for safety, because *of course* you fucking did. Then you had spontaneous, unplanned sex shortly after recovering from cranial surgery, because… hey, why not, right? So, I suppose the question is, did it work? The psychic energy transfer, I mean. It's pretty clear that the sex worked."

Nahleene made a strange, choked-off noise—then cleared her throat.

"It... uh... seems to have done the trick," she said. "I do feel much better now. And my telepathy feels pretty much back to normal."

"*Brilliant*," Ryder said, still in that strangely light tone. "I'm sure you won't mind if I scan both of you to make certain you're not going to start singing show tunes, or spontaneously bleed from the eyeballs or something. After which, we're supposed to meet with the others to discuss what you've told us, Ambassador." She paused. "Though you both might want to shower first."

Nahleene blushed copper, from her neck to the roots of her pale hair. Pax couldn't help thinking it was an appealing look on her.

"That is acceptable," he told Ryder agreeably.

Half a cycle later, Ryder was apparently confident that there was no imminent danger of either unsolicited show tunes or ocular bleeding, and she reluctantly let them both go. Pax escorted Nahleene to a set of unoccupied crew quarters, and from there, to the lav. He noted with interest that the unidentified green slime mold in the left-hand sink had continued to spread during the past few weeks, and was now creeping onto the section of countertop separating it from the right-hand sink.

Fortunately, the mystery mold had not appeared in either the toilet or the cramped shower stall. *Yet*.

"Avoid the green substance, please," he said. "Ryder hasn't been able to positively identify it, and none of our eradication efforts have been successful."

Nahleene edged back a step. "*Nice*. Thanks for the warning... I think."

Pax regarded her, an unaccustomed sense of preoccupation affecting him as he remembered the feeling of her touching him, physically and mentally, pleasure and happiness flowing through him as her mind tangled with his.

He took her hand, skin on skin. It was different than before—not as intense—and he gathered that she was employing mental shielding. Perhaps it also made a difference that only their hands were touching. Still, he could feel the echo of her emotion through the light contact. Surprise. Curiosity.

After a quick assessment regarding the appropriateness of the suggestion, he spoke. "This is transparently selfish on my part. However, it is true that even with recycling, conservation of water resources is important in surroundings such as this."

Nahleene blinked, and her mouth curled into a smile. The emotion leaching through the light contact gained a hint of amusement... a hint of self-consciousness. "Conservation of water resources, huh? You're certain you're not suggesting intimacy as a way to drive home the point that I didn't take advantage of you earlier?"

"You did not take advantage of me earlier," he reiterated. "No more than I will be taking advantage of you, should you agree now that efficient use of the station water supply is an important consideration."

She lifted her free hand, her fingertips brushing over his lips. The brief caress strengthened his sense of her feelings. He found he was fascinated by the process of identifying the emotions as they flashed across his consciousness—so complex and layered. How had he lived so long without them?

"It does sounds like a very important consideration," she murmured. Her eyes widened innocently, and impish wickedness flowed across his mind. "What a pity it's so terribly cramped in there, though. Why, we'll practically be on top of each other."

Pax felt his lips curve into a smile, shaped by the emotions he borrowed from her.

"So we will," he agreed. "I suppose we'll have to make due somehow."

Half a cycle later, Nahleene ran her fingers through her short hair, trying to restore it to some kind of order as it dried. After a shower which turned out not to be quite as efficient—or as focused on cleanliness—as it might have been, she was trying to drag her mind out of the clouds, and back to the markedly less appealing reality of their current situation.

At no point in her life had Nahleene thought, 'Hmm, maybe I should fall for a rogue cyborg soldier with muscles like the statue of an ancient god, and an eight-pack that's every bit as much fun to lick as you'd expect it to be.' Where in the Seven Systems was this behavior even coming from? She was a spy. A *professional*. She didn't *do* things like this.

She shook her head in bewilderment. Where was this coming from? Okay, maybe it was coming from the fact that he'd charged into deadly danger to rescue her, and whisked her away to safety like some romantic hero in a novel. Or that he was in possession of the most unique mind she'd ever touched. Or that he was kind despite having no emotional capacity… or that he cultivated a sense of humor despite having no way to appreciate his own wit.

Yeah, all right. She was clearly screwed at this point. And not just in the fun way, though she'd certainly enjoyed that part all too well.

But now, it was serious time again. Evidently, she was about to meet the remaining members of the vigilante group behind the production and dissemination of the bioweapon antidote in the Ilarian Capital. The question now became how much help they might end up being to each other.

It seemed entirely possible that her position as both an ambassador and a spy would soon be gone forever. Captain Tarell had clearly communicated with someone in a position of power on Ilarius, and told them about her attempt at espionage. Even with her telepathic influence, there would be no putting that information back in its box. Vithara would publicly stand up for her against the Regime on principal, but as soon as they found out about her ties to Maelfian intelligence, they'd privately cut her loose—assuming they didn't try to prosecute her themselves. And, as for the Maelfians? Well, she was no use to anyone as a spy now that her cover had been blown.

Pax ushered her to a door that slid back to reveal an ancient control room. Inside, four Vithii and three humans awaited them. She recognized Kade, Ryder, and the dark-skinned human man from the prison riot immediately. A moment later, she realized that the golden-haired human female must be

Skye Chantrell, the daughter of the scientist who had developed the bio-agent. Depending on who you asked, she had achieved either fame or infamy a few weeks ago, as the face and voice on the pirated vidcast urging humans in the Capital to drink the tap water laced with antitoxin to protect themselves.

All but one of the men stood up as she entered. Kade cleared his throat.

"Ambassador Veila'ana. Ryder said you've recovered. We were just about to discuss the current situation and start coming up with possible strategies." He gestured to his companions one by one. "This is Hunter, Draven, Skye, and Ash. Ryder and Temple, I believe you already know."

The strongly built Vithii with feathered tattoos who'd been introduced as Hunter tipped his chin to her politely, and Nahleene realized with a start that she was standing across from the Rook—perhaps the most wanted man on Ilarius. *Interesting.* Had the propaganda machine turned on a political enemy by unfairly vilifying him as a criminal? Or had a criminal turned to political intrigue for reasons of his own?

She glanced at the others as well, her gaze catching on the olive-skinned human man who hadn't risen. Kade had called him Ash. He gave her a wan smile, but she was struck by the gray cast of his complexion and the dark smudges under his eyes.

"Forgive me for not rising, Ambassador," he said in a smooth, pleasantly accented voice. "I'm afraid I'm under doctor's orders. As you've already met our doctor, I'm certain you'll understand."

She let an answering smile briefly crinkle the corners of her eyes. "Indeed I do. Think nothing of it. And please, call me Nahleene. That goes for all of you. I fear the title of Ambassador may not apply for much longer."

"Nahleene," Hunter said, and she sensed immediately that he was the de facto leader of the group. "Ryder conveyed the gist of your description of the new cyborg program—that the scientists are converting dead Vithii and controlling them using the downloaded minds of decommissioned living cyborgs. Now that you are more fully recovered, do you have anything else to add to that?"

"That's the gist," she said. "They're using the fresh corpses of prisoners slated for execution. Any of them who are deemed physically large and strong enough are brought to the orbital platform and killed on site, so they can go straight onto the slab for cyber enhancement."

The others looked grim, but Skye looked positively ill. "That is utterly and completely barbaric," she said.

"It is," Nahleene agreed, "and the results are every bit as terrifying as you'd imagine. But... I'm not sure you can call it any more repugnant than ripping the free will and emotion from a person's mind while they're still alive."

Skye's summer-blue eyes were pained as she gazed past Nahleene's shoulder, and Nahleene knew she was looking at Pax. "No," she said sadly. "You're absolutely right about that."

Something inside Nahleene's chest warmed at the realization that Pax's friendships with these people were not one-sided. It was clear they valued him for the person he was, and she was glad for that.

It was Pax who spoke next.

"While it's true that the dead cannot suffer any more than what they already suffered during execution, it is the other aspect of this procedure that I find most... troubling. The use of decommissioned cyborg minds."

Ryder nodded. "Yes. I'd wondered if you'd come to the same conclusion I did."

"About the distress call?" Pax asked. "It seems likely."

"What conclusion is that?" Hunter prompted. "Explain."

Pax shifted behind her shoulder. "If my batch-sibling's mind was uploaded into a corpse before being reactivated, his first awareness would have been a condition of catastrophic physical failure. That... is one very obvious reason why a cyborg might activate a distress beacon."

FOURTEEN

Ryder was still nodding at him as Pax outlined his theory on D-8's distress beacon, clearly in agreement with his assessment. It was good to have a working hypothesis that explained the seeming contradiction logically, but it didn't make him any less determined to act on his dead batch-sibling's behalf. The question now became what form that action should take.

"That was my conclusion as well," Ryder confirmed. "Just to be clear, though, you haven't received any other distress beacons? Only D-8's?"

"Correct," he said. "Though there are several possible explanations for that part of it, given this new information. All of the other reanimated cyborgs might have come from different batches, and therefore I would not have been a target for the beacon. The technicians might have reprogrammed the uploaded cyborg minds to discount catastrophic physical failure as a trigger for the beacon. Or they might have altered the enhancement process so that the body is reanimated physically before the full cyborg mind is uploaded to it."

"That makes sense," Hunter said. "Perhaps we should now shift focus to our next steps. Ambassador… Nahleene. I'd like to begin with you. We have the ability to send moderately secure transmissions from the station. You've been understandably discreet about offering details regarding your activities beyond the scope of your primary diplomatic role for Vithara. But if you need to contact any extra-planetary parties about recent events, you can speak to Kade or Ash about it."

"Thank you," Nahleene said, sounding grim. "I do at least need to contact Vithara. I can discuss the details with them once we're done here."

Hunter nodded and turned his gaze to Pax. "Next question. What, if anything, are we going to do about these new developments in the cyborg program?"

Pax did not hesitate. "I intend to destroy the reanimated cyborgs—and, ideally, the developers' means to make more."

"How?" Skye beat the rest of them to the question.

He tilted his head. "That is something I hope to determine with input from all of you during this and future meetings."

Nahleene turned to look up at him with pale eyes. "It sounds like a suicide mission, Pax."

He blinked, her words causing an idea to click into place in his mind. He set it aside for the moment, wanting to make her understand. "The minds of my fellow cyborgs are being corrupted. Exploited. They were living beings once, no different than myself. I may have no ethical argument proving that the cyber-enhancement of reanimated cadavers is worse than the cyber-enhancement of live Vithii, but I will not stand by while my dead siblings' minds are used to enable the process."

He and Nahleene continued to stare at each other, and Pax found himself wishing for physical contact so that he might better understand what she was feeling.

Ryder's voice broke the moment. "Do we know what form these uploaded minds take? You speak of ethical implications, Pax—but do we know whether these recorded… *memories*, for lack of a better term, have any form of sentience or consciousness remaining?"

Nahleene swallowed and turned her attention away from Pax. "According to what I was told before I was detained, the benefit of using dead minds controlled by AI is that there is no possibility of free will returning. They were described to me as mindless automatons."

"The cyborg I encountered showed no indication of awareness of self," Pax said, remembering dead eyes and mindless compliance with orders. He paused, weighing his next words. "And if somehow, a flicker of my fellow cyborgs still exists behind electronic code, I would seek to destroy them regardless. They have been victimized, and put to a morally reprehensible use. It is clear that, trapped in a dead mind, the chance of them regaining even the sort of life I have regained is essentially zero."

There was a stretch of thoughtful silence as the others digested his words.

Kade cleared his throat. "That's all well and good, but what possible method could we implement to destroy dozens of undead cyborgs? Even a single cyborg is damned hard to kill—that's rather the point of them. And I don't know about you, but I have no intention of trying to storm that orbital facility with a couple of two-seat fighters and some hand blasters. It'd be laughable even if they *weren't* on high alert after our little stunt a couple of days ago."

"Direct military assault is off the table," Hunter said seriously. "I'm certain you realize how impractical it would be, Pax—probably better than I do. So, do you have an alternative proposal?"

"A virus," Pax said simply.

Ryder raised an eyebrow. "I assume you don't mean the biological kind," she said.

Ash sighed. "No, he means the other kind."

Pax nodded. "Without a living organic brain, the reanimated cyborgs are entirely dependent on software. Shut it down, and they become corpses once more... albeit corpses with bloodstreams full of bots."

"You want to wipe the hard drive," Ash clarified.

"Correct," Pax said.

"Method of infection?" Ash asked.

"Preferably remote."

"Fucking hell, Pax," Ash said.

But Pax shook his head. "There is an obvious delivery mechanism. I experienced it myself."

Kade lifted an eyebrow. "The distress beacon, you mean? Hmm. That's not a half-bad idea."

"What about the distress beacon?" Temple asked, frowning.

"Oh," Ryder said. "I get it. Kade's right. That's *not* a half-bad idea. Design the software virus to attach copies of itself to a cyborg's distress beacon. As soon as the AI starts undergoing a cascade failure and shutdown, it triggers the distress beacon, spreading the virus to every other cyborg that receives the call. It seems logically sound. Is it feasible from a programming perspective, *leetha*?"

Ash tapped a finger against his lips. Pax noted the signs of exhaustion still evident in the human's slumped shoulders and dark-smudged eyes, but his expression had already changed to the inward-looking one that said he was writing code in his head.

"Depends," he said eventually. "First, can I clone your system architecture, Pax? Is there enough spare memory on this old hulk of a station to download a mirror of it so I can tinker?"

"Yes to both," Pax said.

"And second, do we have any way of knowing whether the new cyborgs are using that same basic architecture beneath the AI?" Ash asked.

"We do," Pax said. "I was only able to overpower the reanimated cyborg guarding the transport by linking to its systems. That gave me the ability to override its command codes using emergency protocols. Those codes and protocols worked as expected."

Ash lifted his eyebrows and shot him a quick, tight smile. "That was quick thinking, big man," he said approvingly. "Brains before brawn, eh? Yes, that's a good indication that they haven't changed any of the important bits. Sounds like cyborg version 2.0 is still backwards compatible."

"So you can do this?" Hunter asked.

Ash shrugged. "I'll have to take a look at what I get from Pax. But, in theory, yes. It's not even that complicated of a build. Erasing things wholesale is a lot easier than, oh, say, reprogramming an airlock maintenance program to unlock doors in a completely unrelated system." The last part was delivered rather pointedly, and Pax gathered it was meant as some sort of backhanded commentary about the prison riot that he and Draven engineered to rescue Ryder not long ago.

Nahleene let out a surprised laugh. "Prophets, that thing with the door locks in the prison was *you*? Remind me not to piss you off."

Ash waved the words away. "Oh, not to worry. People around here piss me off all the time. Just ask anyone." He grew serious. "Pax, let me know when you want to start. I'll need to clear out a partition in the outpost's database so I can work, but that shouldn't take long."

Draven had been quiet up until that point, but now he met Pax's eyes. "This doesn't help with getting the virus to the cyborgs in the first place, though. You can't transmit it remotely to the first one. You'll have to get up close and personal to upload it, which still sounds like a good way for someone to get killed."

Pax straightened. "There is time to consider the strategy for initial delivery while Ash is working on the virus itself."

Hunter shifted. "Yes, that's true enough. Let's get started. Kade, would you help the ambassador set up whatever confidential communiqués she needs to send?"

Kade grunted. "On it. There's a communications relay room we can use, where we won't be underfoot while Pax and Ash are busy sniping at each other."

Nahleene glanced over her shoulder at Pax again, giving him a small smile. Her fingers brushed the back of his hand, and a wave of affection washed over him. He caught his breath, and wondered if anyone else in the room had noticed.

"I'll be back soon," Nahleene said softly.

He nodded wordlessly.

"Ryder," Hunter began, "is Ash all right to work?"

Ash pinned the leader with a dark gaze. "*Don't*, Hunter. I get enough of that shit from the others. I don't need it from you, too."

Ryder shrugged. "If he's well enough to snarl at you, he's probably well enough to sit in a chair and stare at computer code," she said, unperturbed.

Draven looked ready to jump into the fray, so Pax interrupted before the argument could escalate. "Do you prefer to work here or in the computer core, Ash?" he asked, cutting off whatever Draven had drawn breath to say.

"I daresay the computer core will be quieter," Ash replied, biting off the words.

Pax shrugged and indicated they should go, ushering the human into the corridor ahead of him. He was at least moving better, Ryder's medical repairs to his damaged kidney apparently having done their job.

"They're only worried, Ash," he observed, once they were out of earshot of the control room.

"And what good does their worry do me, Pax?" Ash asked, lacing the words with bitter irony. "Please do me a favor and stick to playing armchair psychologist with Ryder. It actually helps her when you do it. It does *not* help me."

Pax was silent.

After a moment, Ash sighed. "Sorry. I suppose I should wait until you do something genuinely irritating before I start in on you." He squared his shoulders, changing conversational tack. "So. You and the ambassador, eh? Can't say I saw that one coming."

The door to the computer core loomed just ahead. Pax looked down at his companion, contemplating the events of the last day. "Nor did I," he said truthfully.

Ash snorted, and palmed the door sensor. It slid open. "She seems a good sort. Though I suppose I don't have to tell you that you want to watch yourself when it comes to spies. Short-tempered, untrustworthy sods, the lot of us."

"That has not been my experience to date," Pax said, "but I appreciate the warning nonetheless."

Nahleene poked her head into the room containing the outpost's computer core some time later, only to find the human, Ash, attaching wire leads to a port on Pax's facial implant. Even though Pax was seated rather than laid out on a slab, his closed eyes and blank expression were enough to make her shiver as she remembered the same thing being done to the cyborgs on the orbital platform.

"Mad scientist at work, do not disturb?" she asked with forced lightness, pushing the image away.

Ash glanced up and shot her a crooked smile. "Merely a mad computer programmer and occasional techworm, I'm afraid. Come on in, though. Pax is partly powered down so I can get past his firewalls—don't mind him. It gives us the perfect opportunity to gossip about him."

Pax's eyes opened. "The operative word in 'partly powered down' is *partly*, Ash," he said, and Nahleene couldn't help the laugh that slipped out.

His eyes slid over her for a moment, softening. Then he closed them again.

"Oh, my. I guess that's me told," Ash said. "Seriously, though, pull up a seat if you're staying. Did Kade get you sorted as far as the comms?"

Nahleene grabbed a molded duraplast chair and made herself comfortable, the unremitting tension coiled in her chest loosening a bit as her body seemed to decide that they'd hit a short reprieve between crises.

"Yes," she said, taking the opportunity to shamelessly study Pax's strong features, now that his eyes were closed again. "I sent a message to the Vitharan government giving them a slightly edited version of recent events—including what I saw on the platform before I was detained. I think it's best if I don't attempt any additional communications just now."

"Mm-hmm." Ash was obviously splitting his attention between her words and what he was doing with Pax's systems, but he threw her another knowing glance. "Balancing competing obligations can be a royal bitch, as I'm painfully aware."

It was clear that there were quite a few undercurrents between Ash and the others on the station to which she wasn't privy, but for now, Nahleene didn't pry.

"It can," she agreed. "I made a point of being quite vague about my current location, of course, but I imagine someone from Vithara will eventually want to arrange a rendezvous so they can pick me up and take me home."

Pax's eyes opened again, but she didn't meet them this time. She wasn't ready yet to think about that particular part of *what came next*. Not when it almost certainly involved her being far, far away from the Vithii cyborg seated next to the computer core.

"And is that likely to cause a problem for you?" Ash asked, still giving the appearance that most of his attention was focused on the screen in front of him.

"I have no idea," she said. "There are some other options available to me, though, if it comes to it."

The smartest of those options would probably be to make a run for Maelfius. The government there would make at least a token effort not to allow her to be extradited to either Ilarius or Vithara. Would that effort stand up to serious pressure? She wasn't sure. A chill of unease went through her at the thought that the Regime might use her as an excuse to ratchet up tensions with the Maelfians.

Her mission here had been to head off possible conflict between the two worlds. Would she unintentionally end up hastening it instead?

But the Ilarian government had no proof that she was spying for Maelfius. They would only have suspicions based on her dual parentage. If anything, they would be more likely to blame Vithara… unless she ran straight to Maelfius for asylum. That would be a bit of a giveaway, she imagined.

"Okay, here we go," Ash said, typing rapidly. "I need two copies to work on, so this is going to be a tight fit for the available station memory. Think digitally compressed thoughts, Pax."

Nahleene snorted, drawn away from her dark thoughts by the banter. Lines of data flashed across the screen too fast for her to follow.

"This isn't a full download," Ash said, flicking a glance her way. "Nothing like what the tech-heads are doing at the R&D facility. I'm only interested in the file architecture, not the data inside the files. Even so, it's a devilishly complex system. It never would have been practical before nano-computing."

Curious, Nahleene asked, "Speaking of that, what about the bots? Does the implanted tech control them, too?"

"Sort of," Ash replied absently. "Besides the cranial implant, there's a second implant in the chest. The body's entire blood supply is filtered through that one, and it's responsible for catching any rogue or deactivated bots. It can also reprogram them on the fly if more specialized ones are needed. The two implants communicate, but the cranial implant does the executive-level stuff, while the chest implant is more for implementation and quality control."

"An overly simplistic explanation," Pax said, not opening his eyes.

"Shush," Ash retorted. "Don't talk back when I'm downloading you." He lifted an eyebrow, still typing commands in a rapid clatter of keystrokes. "Anyway, Ryder's the bot expert here. I just sling code. Honestly, sometimes I find it amazing that nanotech hasn't gone rogue and killed us all before now. It's fucking terrifying stuff."

"Only to meatbags," Pax muttered.

Ash made a skeptical noise. "If you say so. But just remember, if one of those little creatures ever pops a covalent bond and starts multiplying out of control, you'll be the first to collapse into a puddle of voracious gray goo."

Nahleene winced. "Yeah, not really a visual I needed, thanks."

"Sorry," Ash said, sounding distracted again. The data streaming across the screen came to an abrupt stop, a cursor flashing green at the bottom. "Right... looks like we might have to take a rain check on the gossip. I've got what I need, Pax—you can power up again."

Pax reached up and unclipped the leads from the metal implant along his cheek and forehead. "I want to speak further with Hunter, assuming you're done with me for now, Ash." He caught her eye. "I'd hoped you would accompany me to that meeting as well, Nahleene."

"Love to," Nahleene said, already dying to know more about the reasons why the infamous Rook appeared to be more interested in engineering a political coup than engaging in the mayhem and violent crime he'd so often been accused of.

"Go on, then, both of you," Ash said. "Scram, and let me work. I'll call you when I have anything worth reporting."

"Very well," Pax said, rising and crossing to join her by the door. "Try to remember that the human body requires nourishment and rest at regular intervals. It all sounds terribly tiresome, but I've been reliably informed it's necessary."

Ash slowed in his typing long enough to flash a middle finger in Pax's direction, not bothering to look up from the screen. Nahleene huffed a silent breath of amusement, and let Pax herd her out of the door.

FIFTEEN

They found Hunter and Skye Skye still in the control room. It hadn't taken Nahleene very much time at all to figure out the two of them were a couple, and that made her even more intrigued by the dynamics of what was going on here.

Pax indicated a chair, and she realized that she was, in fact, growing tired already, even though she'd only been awake for a few cycles at most. She gave him a grateful nod and sat. Apparently, having cranial surgery twice in the space of two days really took it out of you, psychic healing abilities or no.

Who knew?

"Ambassador," Hunter said. "I'm glad you and Pax returned. I'd like to talk in more depth about the political situation elsewhere in the Seven Systems. It's become increasingly difficult to get accurate information on Ilarius, thanks to the government's stranglehold on the news media. And while there are other underground sources, they also tend to carry a decided slant."

She debated reminding Hunter to call her Nahleene again, but decided it wasn't worth it. "I can at least speak to the situation on Vithara, though you probably won't like what I have to say."

Skye looked sour. "They never seemed to have much interest in Ilarius beyond making sure the trade balance with us was tilted in their favor. I'm guessing that hasn't changed."

Nahleene met her blue gaze frankly. "The relationship between Vithara and the Vithii on Ilarius has always been complicated. It may have ended more than a century ago, but people on both sides of the divide still have strong opinions about the civil war. Many back home on Vithara consider the people who originally fled to Ilarius to be war criminals. They find the rise of the Regime... unsurprising. Just a return to form, basically."

"That's such bullshit," Skye said, sounding tired. "We had peace on Ilarius for almost a hundred years before things started going to hell. And it's not like *all* Vithii are anti-human. I don't think it's even a majority. The ones who are anti-human just happen to be really loud and well organized."

"Such is the case in most repressive regimes throughout history," Pax said.

"True enough," Nahleene agreed readily. "But the practical upshot is, while people on Vithara feel bad—even outraged—about what's happening to the humans on Ilarius, there's no public mandate for the government to try to play interstellar policeman."

Hunter regarded her thoughtfully. "Is there any will to enact economic sanctions, or other non-military forms of censure?"

"Not really," she said with sincere regret.

"Would that be likely to change if the ambassador from Terra Nova started lobbying the Vitharan leaders for action?" he asked, still watching her closely.

Nahleene blinked. Terra Nova was the largest of the human colonies that had sprung up after the

Great Diaspora, and the only other notable concentration of humans in the Seven Systems besides Ilarius.

"Terra Nova has expressed neutrality, except for its offer of asylum to humans fleeing the Regime," she said carefully. "What you're describing would be a distinct about-face in policy."

"Yes," Hunter said. "It would. But, if it were to occur?"

All three sets of eyes in the room were watching her with interest.

"I... don't really know," she said honestly. "It would certainly shift the balance in the local star cluster." She paused, not quite ready to delve into her exact relationship with the Maelfian government. Best to keep things non-specific for now. "Some of the other planets that aren't military powers in their own rights are getting nervous. If Terra Nova set itself directly against the Regime, they might pile on in hopes of gaining the military support of a coalition."

"And if all of the other systems united, and started putting pressure on Vithara to act?" Skye pressed, leaning forward in her chair.

"Political pressure is a powerful force," Nahleene said. "I take it this means you know something I don't about the Terra Novan ambassador?"

It was Hunter who answered. "Let's just say that there is an attempt underway to gain her ear. There are no guarantees, obviously."

She could hardly blame Hunter for holding back and being vague, since she was doing exactly the same thing to him. She did find it interesting that Skye appeared to be biting the inside of her cheek to keep herself from saying something—and judging by her expression, whatever she was holding back was a subject she found upsetting.

Nahleene itched to dart across the distance separating them and read the pair's minds, but that would have been a considerable breach of trust under the current circumstances. If they were going to become allies, they'd need to build this relationship the old-fashioned way. She just hoped they'd have time to do so.

"I don't know if the Terra Novan ambassador having a change of heart would be enough to tip the balance in favor of intervention on Ilarius or not," she said eventually. "But it would certainly be a start. And I hope it goes without saying that I will help in any way I can, as long as it doesn't harm the interests of those I'm sworn to serve."

"I understand," Hunter said.

"I'm not sure you do," she told him. "But, unfortunately, there's a real question about how much power I have to help anyone, now—myself included. I may be about to become a fugitive myself, if that ends up being the best way for me to protect those interests I just mentioned."

Because she refused to be responsible for turning the Premiere's attention—and his aggression—toward Maelfius. Not if she could possibly help it. Nor did she have any real desire to end up imprisoned on Vithara for being a double agent. Right now, it was looking more and more like she was about to be in the same situation as everyone else on this outpost. Idly, she glanced at Pax and wondered if Hunter's crew had a position open for a half-breed telepath with a degree in communications and another in interplanetary relations.

Pax sat in the canteen with Nahleene, eating a meal with her after leaving the impromptu strategy session with Hunter and Skye. Normally, he would consume whatever raw nutrients his body needed without ceremony—fat, protein, simple sugars, and whatever vitamins and minerals were necessary—preferably in pill form. However, his system was more than capable of processing normal foodstuffs, and he found that in Nahleene's company, the thought appealed more than it normally would.

Nahleene had seemed distracted ever since speaking with Hunter. He suspected she was worrying about the repercussions of having been caught spying and outed as a telepathic Maelfian hybrid. It was understandable. While diplomatic immunity would have protected her in any surroundings where the rule of law was paramount, it was clear that the Regime was more interested in their own security than in interstellar convention.

"You are concerned about the future," he said, watching her push the remains of her half-eaten meal around the tray.

She huffed in amusement. "I'm concerned about many things. But, yes, the future is one of those things."

"You fear that the Regime has communicated information about you to Vithara that may be damaging?" he asked.

She put down her utensils. "I'd be surprised if they haven't, honestly." She sighed. "The Vitharan government knows my mother is Maelfian... but they don't know I'm a telepath. My parents were very careful not to advertise that fact as I was growing up. They instilled in me from an early age that being a telepath would be an advantage to me in my adult life, but that letting other Vitharans *know* I was a telepath would make me an outsider, greatly limiting my future options."

"I had wondered if the Vitharan government was aware of your abilities," he said.

"No. It wasn't. I doubt I ever would have been granted an ambassadorship if anyone had been aware. There would be too many opportunities for diplomatic misunderstandings if the host planet found out the Vitharan ambassador could pluck thoughts directly from their heads... as we've recently discovered." She raised a sardonic eyebrow, and muttered, "Not that this was a *misunderstanding*, since I really was trying to influence one of their officials and spy on a secret program."

"You could stay here," Pax said.

The other eyebrow rose. "On an abandoned lunar outpost in the middle of nowhere?"

"With us," he clarified. Though, more accurately, it would be the others she was staying with—not him. And that thought was enough to make his hand itch to cover hers, so he could feel her emotions flowing through him like a warm tide. Unfortunately, doing so right now would be unwise in the extreme.

Her eyebrows lowered, and her gaze locked with his as she said, "There are certainly less appealing options."

He shaped his lips into a smile, and hoped that lack of practice had not turned the expression into anything ridiculous or alarming. Apparently it had not, since her features softened in response.

She took a deep breath and changed the subject. "Have you thought any more about how you might be able to introduce the virus into the reanimated cyborgs?"

"I have," he replied. "There is one possibility with considerable promise, but I'm not quite ready to discuss it with the others yet."

"I wouldn't have pegged a cyborg as being mysterious when it came to discussing military strategy," she teased.

He shrugged. "Until I have the details in place, such a discussion would be counterproductive. And until Ash comes up with working code for me, the point is moot anyway."

Pax set his misgivings about the plan aside, relegating them to the future and focusing on the present. He indulged his earlier selfish urge, and covered her hand with his. She turned her palm over so she could lace their fingers together.

"You are weary," Pax observed. "You should not overexert yourself so soon after your recovery."

She smiled, but it was a wan expression. "Not sure I could sleep right now, to be honest. Too much on my mind."

He thought for a moment. "Perhaps I could make a suggestion, in that case?" he offered.

She looked at him curiously, and let him lead her out of the canteen. He took her to the outer edge of the station. The place was falling into disrepair due to age and neglect, but there was still one significant reminder of its original purpose as a stellar cartography outpost.

The clearsteel observatory dome might have been scratched dull by decades of sand and dust on the windward side, but the other half was still an impressive viewport into the cosmos. At some point during their previous stay, Draven had dragged a battered sofa underneath the expanse of transparent metal. He could often be found there during his off-duty time, but now the room was empty and echoing.

"Wow," Nahleene breathed, moving away from him until she was standing beneath the undamaged area, looking up. He watched her watch the sky, until she finally dragged her eyes away to take in the rest of her surroundings. "I didn't expect anything like this, although I guess I did hear someone say *stellar cartography* earlier. I'm still not sure how much actual rest I'll get, but as places for uninterrupted brooding go, I suppose you can't beat the view."

Pax dusted off the worn cushions on the sofa and sat at one end, firmly pushing away all thoughts of the virus and its dissemination. He was gratified when Nahleene gave him a smile that seemed oddly shy before easing herself down to lie along the couch lengthwise, with her head propped on his thigh.

She sighed, watching the stars wheel slowly above them.

"It's so beautiful... yet sentient beings always seem to be in such a hurry to bring ugliness into it," she said. "War, terror, crime, disease..."

He looked up, unable to see what she saw. Unable to see *anything* other than a random collection of distant, flickering lights. One of her hands reached back blindly, searching for his. He took it, letting her twine their fingers together. A moment later, the beauty of the panorama above them crept over his awareness... a combination of aesthetic and philosophical appreciation. He split his attention between the light of distant stars and the face of the woman resting half in his lap.

It didn't take much consideration to decide which one affected him more.

SIXTEEN

It was several cycles later when a soft chime came over the all-comms system. Despite her protestations, Nahleene had fallen asleep after only a few minutes of stargazing—obviously still feeling the effects of the serious medical procedures she'd undergone.

Pax had remained alert, devoting the time to cataloguing the different emotions that brushed along his awareness as she dreamed. He had the distinct impression he would never get tired of doing that. How odd that he had never really felt the lack before. Or perhaps it wasn't odd—the moment his emotion centers had been burned out, he'd lost the ability to pine for his missing feelings right along with everything else.

Was her telepathic ability somehow forging new pathways within his brain? That was how Ryder thought he'd spontaneously regained his free will several years ago, after all—his neurons rewiring themselves to compensate for damaged areas. It was apparently possible, though he'd certainly never expected such a thing to happen again after so many years.

"Nahleene," he said in a low voice.

She blinked awake, looking blearily around the room. "What's that noise?" she asked, her voice the same low rasp that it had been after he'd pleasured her in the shower. He marveled at the way his cock twitched, searching for her heat—the reaction completely involuntary.

"Ash is paging me with an all-comms call," he explained.

"Oh." She grunted and rolled into a sitting position. "Sorry... I think I drooled on you."

The loss of mental contact as she moved away was jarring.

"I assure you, I've had worse," he told her and rose to respond to the call.

"Pax?" came Ash's tinny voice, once he'd flicked the switch.

"Here," he confirmed. "You have news?"

"I do. I'm about to test the virus on the copies of your file architecture. I've stuffed them with some dummy data. Thought you might want to be here for the experiment, but first we need to make very certain that your receiving system for cyborg distress beacons is locked down tight. The others would probably be cross with me if I accidentally wiped your databanks while I was playing around with this thing."

"That would be unfortunate, yes," he agreed.

Nahleene shifted on the couch behind him. "Is that a real danger?"

"I will shut down my internal receiver before the test," he assured her.

"And I'll send an uninfected distress call from one of the copies just to confirm that it's properly blocked," Ash added. "You might have an organic brain to fall back on, but it's still not something to play around with. For one thing, the sudden destruction of a large part of your mental capacity would probably throw you into a coma, and for another, only the cybertech can direct your bots. I wouldn't like to think what would happen to your body without technological control over the damned things."

It was nothing he hadn't already considered, but it would be a moot point with his receiver powered down for the duration of the test.

"It will not be a problem. I'll be there in five minutes," he said.

"Good. I'll let the others know," Ash said, and signed off.

Nahleene still felt half-asleep as she stumbled after Pax, returning to the computer core where Ash had apparently spent the last several hours inventing a cyborg virus while she'd been napping under the stars. She couldn't help the small shiver at the idea of the thing accidentally infecting Pax, even though they would be taking precautions and he seemed unconcerned by the possibility.

Most of the others had also assembled in the small room, making it seem decidedly crowded. Draven was apparently standing watch in the control center, but Hunter, Skye, Ryder, Temple, and Kade were here to observe the test.

"Are you locked down?" Ash asked Pax without preamble as soon as they entered. "No receiving capabilities on subspace frequencies alpha-zero-one to zed-nine-nine?"

"Yes," Pax assured him.

"Right. One virus-free test transmission headed your way."

Ash flipped a switch, and all eyes focused on Pax.

"Nothing," he confirmed a moment later.

"Good enough," Ash said. "Time to load the live rounds."

For the first time, Nahleene noticed how terrible the human truly looked. He'd appeared weak or ill when she'd first been introduced—she remembered his wan apology for not rising with the others.

Doctor's orders, he'd explained with a shrug.

Now, he looked like a stiff breeze from the ventilation duct would topple him right out of his chair. That didn't take away from the light of determined enthusiasm in his eyes, however. She'd seen the same light in her mother's eyes after completing a particularly challenging engineering proposal, and recognized the look of someone who was both good at what they did and passionate about it.

"I'm going to introduce the virus into the first copy of the cyborg file structure. I've got the second copy partitioned, but both are hooked into the comm system's transmitting and receiving arrays. The distress beacons should work pretty much as they would *in vivo*. So if the virus in the first copy transmits itself to the second copy, we're golden."

His brown eyes flicked to Pax.

"I also made a compressed backup copy of the architecture on a portable hard drive," he added. "So if this version of the virus doesn't work, I won't have to plug you into the wall again to get a fresh copy to work on."

"Good thinking," Pax said.

"All right," Ash said. "No point in faffing around. Here we go."

He plugged a small micro-drive into one of the slots on his terminal, then ran his fingers over the track pad, dragging and dropping a single file.

When he was done, he pulled up what Nahleene assumed was a visual representation of the two copies of the cyborg emulator, separated on the screen by a solid line with the tree-like file structure lit up in orange—the color indicating 'all systems go' in Vitharan and Vithii culture.

What happened next was fast. Much faster than she had expected... not that she'd known quite *what* to expect. Points at one tip of the branched cyborg structure flipped from orange to purple, the color of warning. The failure increased in an expanding cascade. When somewhat over half of the structure was purple, the tip of the topmost branch flashed yellow. The corresponding point on the second copy of the cyborg structure also flashed yellow, as if in reply.

"That's the distress beacon sent and received," Ash said, watching the screen closely.

Nahleene couldn't help it—her eyes flew to Pax, just to be sure. He was fine, of course, watching the screen as intently as everyone else was. Within two minutes flat, both copies were completely purple. A moment later, the screen went dark, and came up with a single error message.

Files unavailable.

"I'd say that's a pretty resounding endorsement," Temple offered from his spot beside the door.

"It appears so," Kade agreed.

"There is one fairly significant logistical problem remaining," Ash said, unplugging the microdrive from its slot. "The original copy has to be manually installed. The encryption around a cyborg's internal receiver is staggering. This only worked because I was sending the virus from one identical transmitter/receiver array to another—they're both essentially Pax. Similarly, once we get it inside a group of connected cyborgs—batch siblings, for instance—it should work because it's piggybacking inside the encrypted system. But getting it to the first one... that's not something I can hack."

"It's a definite problem," said Hunter. "We're still not in any kind of position to gain access to a reanimated cyborg inside the program by force. Especially if we would then need to somehow convince it to download unknown software into its own systems."

"I will consider the matter further and see what potential strategies I can come up with," Pax said. "Thank you for your efforts, Ash."

Ash smiled and tossed him the micro-drive. Pax snatched it neatly out of the air. "That's what I'm here for, big man," he said, and stretched carefully in his chair. Nahleene heard joints crackling, and winced in sympathy. "I must say, it was worth it for the peek inside the technological half of your nog. That's an elegant system you've got there."

Pax raised an eyebrow. "Flattery will get you nowhere," he said, and Ash chuckled.

"Right," Ryder said, pushing away from the edge of the desk she'd been leaning against. "If you're done, I'm rescinding your medical permissions, Ash. Go get some sleep, or else I'll confine you to the medbay and put you on a drip feed with a sedative in it."

"Hmph. Well, far be it from me to ignore medical advice," Ash said. Ryder gave an indelicate snort, which he ignored, rising a bit unsteadily.

"Skye," Ryder said, "make sure the idiot gets back to his quarters, will you?"

"Sure," Skye said. "We can raid the canteen for something to eat along the way."

Nahleene was a bit surprised that Ryder had asked the willowy human woman to do the job, instead of any of the hulking Vithii men who could probably carry Ash under one arm without straining themselves. No one else seemed inclined to comment, however.

Pax spoke before the pair reached the door.

"Before you leave," he said, "I wish to convey my appreciation to you all for your willingness to assist me in dealing with this matter." He met the eyes of everyone in the room, one by one. "It is one of the many things I value about our association."

Several of the others looked faintly surprised by the declaration. After a slight pause, Hunter spoke.

"We may be House by choice rather than blood, Pax—but we are still House. We stand together in all things—you know that."

Nahleene noticed the way Temple snuck an arm around Ryder's shoulders, tugging her closer against his side.

Kade shifted. "Honestly. Where's a tissue when you need one?" he deadpanned. "Don't go soft on me now, Pax. I can't be the only cynical bastard on this station."

He made for the door, and that seemed to be the signal for the gathering to break up. Pax pocketed the micro-drive with the virus on it and turned to Nahleene.

"Would you dine with me again?" he asked.

Her smile was heartfelt. "Of course I would."

She let him escort her to the canteen, where Hunter, Temple, Kade, and Ryder were sitting down at a table together when they came in. Rather than joining them, though, Pax loaded food onto a tray and they took it back to the quarters he'd showed her earlier. She gathered the room was hers for the duration of her stay, and once again, thoughts of the future began to clamor for her attention.

Pax set the tray down on a small table. There was only one chair in the room, but he disappeared down the hall and reappeared a moment later with a second one. She was surprised at how hungry she was, and they ate in comfortable silence for a few minutes before Pax pushed the empty Redimeal packaging away.

"I am scheduled for watch duty shortly, but I wished to have a few more minutes alone with you before I left," he said.

Those simple words probably shouldn't have made something in her stomach flutter, but they were just... so... *unexpected*, coming from a cyborg.

"I'm glad you did," she said, the words emerging a bit breathily. This entire situation was far enough outside of her expectations and experience that she wasn't quite sure how to approach it.

He tilted his head, regarding her. "Have you given any more thought to what you will do now?"

That brought reality crashing back down. "Plenty. Which isn't to say that I've come up with any good answers."

He nodded. "It is a complicated situation. You must do whatever is best for the interests you represent, while also keeping yourself safe. I merely wanted to reiterate that remaining with our group is an option. No matter what happens, you will be welcome here with my friends—either temporarily or permanently."

She frowned at his wording. Too many years spent around the diplomatic corps had made her overly sensitive to phrasing and context. And something about this particular phrasing... made it sound like he was trying to distance himself from her personally while still making it clear that his earlier offer of asylum remained open.

"I will... definitely keep that in mind," she said, couching her reply in the same careful terms.

Had she misread things? Was she projecting feelings onto Pax that he could not possibly possess? At what point had she started to see what was between them in terms of *feelings*, anyway? He was a cyborg, for all that he was an extraordinary one. Any feelings here were, by definition, all on her side. Perhaps she'd been reading other things into it based on his behavior toward his friends.

You conflate feeling compassion with understanding compassion. Interesting, he'd observed, early in their admittedly brief acquaintance.

Had she also been conflating his capacity to understand attraction with his capacity to feel it? *Shit.*

He was speaking again. "Nahleene, your ability to share the experience of emotion with me through touch has been an unexpected and priceless gift. I thought you should know that."

His hand covered hers, but, as usual, all she could read from him was his assessment of the current moment. It matched precisely with what he'd just said—he recognized the value of what he'd received through their telepathic contact, and felt it was important that he convey this to her. She stared into his eyes, wishing rather desperately that she could see deeper. The only time she'd managed it with him was when she'd entered into a full link without shields shortly after she'd woken from surgery, and the casual contact of his hand on hers wasn't nearly enough for that.

Before she could decide whether to push the issue... whether to ask outright if he wanted to pursue what they seemed to have started over the past couple of days, he rose.

"My duty shift begins in five minutes," he said. "Otherwise, I would stay longer."

Rather than release her hand, however, he lifted her wrist to his lips, palm up. Teeth closed on the sensitive skin, his eyes never leaving hers as he sucked a Vitharan love mark to the surface. Desire slammed into Nahleene's belly, taking her breath away at the same time it took away her ability to form coherent sentences like, *"Did you really just do that?"* and *"Dear gods, I am so fucking confused right now."*

"To remember me by," he said as he pulled away, a crooked quirk of a smile pulling at one side of his mouth. Then he was out the door before she could regain the power of speech, presumably hurrying for his duty assignment.

"Oh... *shit*," she whispered, staring down at the livid mark.

Pax entered the control room where Draven waited for him to take over watch duty for the remainder of the station night shift. As expected, they were alone, since the watch only required whoever was there to keep an eye on the long-range sensors and monitor the external comms.

Draven looked up at the sound of the doors opening and stretched. "Oh, good. You're here. Nothing to report, as you might've guessed. Dead quiet out there tonight."

Pax nodded. "Actually, Draven, I have a favor to ask," he said.

Surprise flickered across Draven's heavy features. "Seriously? A favor? Someone make a note of the time and date. I don't believe you've ever asked me for one of those before." He crossed his arms and leaned back in the molded plastic chair. "So, what can I do for you?"

"I need to devote my full attention to a strategy that will allow me to infect one of the reanimated cyborgs with the virus Ash programmed," he said truthfully. "It is an unfortunate fact that the virus cannot be delivered by low-risk methods. Will you take my watch so I can focus all of my resources on the problem?"

Draven's eyebrows climbed up, but he smoothed his expression a moment later. "Yeah, sure, Pax. I can do that. You're really freaked about this cyborg thing, aren't you? Which, don't get me wrong—I can totally understand. The whole idea is fucking terrifying."

"Thank you," Pax said. "It is true I'd prefer to enact a solution to this issue as soon as possible."

Draven shrugged. "Well, then. Let me worry about watching for stray space dust over the next few cycles. You go come up with a cunning plan. Comm me if there's anything else I can do to help."

Pax laid a hand on Draven's shoulder and squeezed lightly. "Your offer to cover my watch is sufficient. Goodbye, Draven."

Draven looked at him curiously for a moment. "'Night, Pax," he said, before going back to his sensor readouts.

Pax took the micro-drive to the observatory dome. He let the door close behind him but did not lock it. With Nahleene in her quarters and Draven in the control room, he was unlikely to be interrupted for the few minutes it would take him to enact his plan.

There was no scenario in which attempting to capture or otherwise temporarily restrain a reanimated cyborg would not put whoever undertook the mission at substantial risk, and with only a small chance of ultimate success. There was, however, a very obvious and essentially foolproof method of dealing with the situation.

D-8's downloaded mind had been used to reanimate a dead cyborg. Pax and D-8 were batch-siblings, and their distress beacons were still demonstrably linked, since Pax had received a transmission from D-8 on Ilarius. The range of the distress beacon over subspace was system-wide, since anything less than that would be of limited usefulness during inter-system battle. Therefore, Pax could transmit the virus to the cyborg unit containing D-8's memories by means of his own distress beacon, and that unit would spread it to the other reanimated cyborgs.

Simple. Straightforward.

Of course, the others would never permit the attempt, knowing that it would probably also be lethal to Pax. But Pax had always known that there were hills worth dying on. He had also come to have a much keener appreciation over the past few days of what his life could never again be.

The hints of stolen emotion Nahleene had unwittingly given him had been a gift, just as he had told her. They were also a taunt. Nahleene had reached for him out of desperation when her mental abilities were damaged and raw. She had been kind to him. Given him a glimpse of what might have been. But she was an organic and he was a cyborg. She would not wish to tie herself to him long-term. At best, he'd been a temporary shelter for her. At worst, he'd been a mere curiosity.

What could he possibly offer her as a lover? His greatest value had always been as a killer, and it appeared he would be going out in the act of doing just that.

Pax seated himself on the battered couch beneath the observation dome, and swung his legs up to settle comfortably along its length so he could watch those perplexing flickers of distant light while the virus did its work inside his mind. He spared a last thought for those he would be leaving behind. It was regrettable that his actions would cause them distress, but there had never been any question that what they were doing would result in loss of life. He was confident they would continue to support each other without him, and focus on doing what needed to be done.

He examined the micro-drive containing the single file that comprised the virus for a long moment before lifting it to his temple, where he inserted the needle-shaped connector into the appropriate socket in his facial implant. His internal systems recognized the drive, and he initiated the file transfer with barely a flicker of thought.

It was not a large file—testament to Ash's efficiency as a programmer. Once he'd copied it into the appropriate system folder, he opened the .exe extension to make the virus active. Then he turned his attention to the distant stars overhead, intending to contemplate what it was that made them so intriguing to emotional beings while he waited.

Instead, he found himself remembering the way Nahleene's face had looked as she came apart in his arms, and the way her fingers felt on the side of his face as her mind entwined with his. He was still thinking of her when the pain hit, his distress beacon activating automatically as catastrophic systems failure dragged him down into darkness.

SEVENTEEN

Nahleene spent a couple of cycles after Pax left trying to distract herself from her confused thoughts. She started by reading a book on human archaeology from the station's database, before nagging fatigue convinced her to move to the bunk. There, she dozed for some time, jerking awake at intervals in response to nebulous, unnerving dreams.

Eventually, with the chrono reading oh-three-hundred in flashing red numbers, she gave up on getting any kind of restful sleep in the unfamiliar and claustrophobic crew quarters. Perhaps she'd have better luck elsewhere—someplace with more pleasant associations. She ran her fingers through her hair in a half-hearted attempt to make herself presentable in case she ran into anyone in the corridors, then pulled on her boots and headed toward the observation dome where Pax had taken her the previous day.

She took a couple of wrong turnings into unfamiliar areas, but managed to find the door to the observation room after only a few minutes. It opened to her palm print, making her wonder if Pax had added her biometrics to the system at some point, or if they simply weren't big on internal security here since everyone clearly trusted each other.

Her attention went immediately to the arresting view of eternity visible above her. It was only when she approached the old sofa where she'd napped so contentedly with her head on Pax's lap that she noticed the body lying there. The only lighting came from the stars overhead, but they glinted off a fine filigree of metal on the figure's face.

Several thoughts tumbled over each other, trying to reconcile the vision before her.

He... must have come here and fallen asleep?
But he was supposed to be on duty.
And... cyborgs didn't sleep. Did they?

An awful sinking feeling started in her chest and spread to her stomach, making it churn.

"Pax?" she whispered. Then, louder, "Pax. *Pax!*"

She fell to her knees beside the sofa, her hand gripping his bicep beneath the cuff of his short-sleeved black shirt. He did not respond, and her mind encountered only a low background whisper, like barely audible white noise in the distance.

"No, no, no," she moaned, panic clawing at her heart. "*Lights, one hundred percent!*"

The sudden glare of recessed lighting from the workstations made everything so much worse. No longer was the dome a magical space illuminated by starlight. Now, it was a dingy lab with patches of rust flowering on the walls, and a threadbare couch in the middle with a pale, waxen body sprawled over it.

The harsh light glinted on a small, gunmetal gray cylinder jutting from Pax's temple, and sick understanding settled over her like a smothering blanket. *The micro-drive.*

Nahleene lunged for the workstation where she'd seen Pax reply to an all-comms call after the chimes woke her up. For a moment, her brain couldn't decipher the confusion of buttons and switches, but then her eyes settled on a comm speaker and the controls next to it. She pounced on the all-comms button, mashing it down.

"Ryder! *Anyone*! I'm in the observation dome. I need help! It's Pax, he's unresponsive—hurry, *please*!"

Her heart pounded in her ears as the silence stretched. Then, a tightly controlled female Vithii voice, raspy with interrupted sleep.

"I'm on my way. Hunter, are you on this comm?"

"Yes, I'm here, Ryder."

"Get me a stretcher and two people strong enough to carry an unconscious cyborg."

"We'll be right there."

A tiny sliver of relief at the prospect of help arriving threaded through Nahleene's blind panic. She ran back and slid to her knees next to the couch again. This time, she splayed fingers over Pax's face, rather than his arm. There was barely any sense of him—just that confused tangle of whispered nonsense, almost too far away to hear. She strained deeper, trying to find a hint of awareness, and only distantly registered the sound of the door screeching open.

Bare feet slapped the deck plates, and then Ryder was skidding to a halt next to her. She scrabbled in a portable medikit and came up with a scanner, her face almost as pale as Pax's.

"What did he do?" she demanded. "*Tell me what he did.*"

Nahleene pulled her hand away from Pax's face and pointed a shaky finger at the micro-drive protruding obscenely from his implant. "The virus," she whispered.

Ryder went very still for a beat. "Get Ash," she said. "Get him here *now*."

Nahleene lunged for the comms again, but Ash was already on his way. He arrived at the same time as Hunter and Kade with the stretcher.

"Ash," Ryder snapped, "he used the virus on himself. You were mucking around with his systems architecture yesterday, so you're our best bet. Do we have *any* options here?"

The human's olive complexion went chalky and he caught himself against the doorframe. "Pax, you fucking *bastard. Godsdamnit!*" he practically snarled.

"*Ash!*" Ryder snapped. "Options!"

Ash tangled a hand in his dark hair, fisting it as he visibly tried to engage his brain rather than his emotions. "Fuck, fuck… let me think. The data in his cyborg brain is gone—no getting it back. We need some way to regulate his bots. I've got the backup copy of the file architecture I downloaded from him. Can you put him on life support while we try to cobble together a skeleton system to keep his physical body regulated?"

"I can try," Ryder said grimly.

"But what about his mind?" Nahleene asked, trying not to think about the confused whisper that was all she could feel from him now.

"Half of it's gone," Ash said in a flat tone. "The organic half—which may or may not be left—won't do him much good if he undergoes multiple organ failure."

"He's undergoing multiple organ failure *now*," Ryder said. "He must have been like this for hours.

Hunter. Kade. Help me get him on the damned stretcher."

Nahleene stood to one side, hugging herself, fighting the urge to elbow her way past the others and try to reach his mind again. They were right. She knew that, intellectually. She had to let them work to save his body, or nothing else would matter.

After the others rushed Pax to the medbay and hooked him up to emergency life support, Ryder more or less shoved Nahleene out the door and warned her not to come back until someone came to fetch her. She'd spent the intervening several cycles alternately pacing and sitting in the canteen, neither of which did a single fucking thing to calm her down.

Temple and Skye were currently sitting with her, either because they were trying to be nice or because Ryder had told them to make sure she didn't attempt to force her way in to see Pax while she and Ash were still working on him.

"This sucks," Nahleene said. She was currently slumped in an uncomfortable chair with her elbows resting on the canteen table and her head in her hands. "I didn't sign up for any of this shit when I agreed to snoop around the fucking cyborg program for you people. Why would Pax do this?"

"I don't know, and I'm afraid you're going to have to stand in line to kick his ass when he wakes up," Skye said. "The queue forms on the left."

"If he wakes up, you mean," Nahleene muttered.

"He'll wake up," Skye insisted.

"It's hard to be one of the people stuck waiting outside the door," Temple offered, sympathy clear in his tone. "Skye and me, we're pretty good at shooting things, and we can fly most shuttles and small extra-atmospheric craft. She can even offer corporate and non-profit tax advice if you need it. But for shit like this? We're useless."

"Yup," Skye agreed. "I was stuck heating up Redi-meals and getting drinks for the others while they were developing the antidote to the Premiere's bio-weapon... and my *own dad* invented the damned thing. That stung. So I know how you feel."

"That's the thing, though," Nahleene said, lifting her head. She let her right arm fall to the table, palm up, staring at the love bite Pax had left on the inside of her wrist. "I *can* help. I can try to bring his mind back. I owe him that. He let me use his psychic energy to heal myself after the technicians on the orbital station put that implant in my skull."

Skye cocked her head, her eyes fixing on the livid mark. "And is that the only reason you want to help him? Tit for tat because he helped you first?"

Nahleene let her head fall back in her hand, kneading at the pounding headache that was growing behind her eyes. "No. It's not the only reason."

Skye was quiet for a moment before she spoke. "I thought there must be more going on," she said softly. "I've never seen Pax act like that before."

"Act like what?" Nahleene asked, not looking up.

"Like he was smitten," Skye clarified.

"I don't want to talk about this right now," she said, a bit of desperation creeping into her tone.

"Okay," Skye told her. "I'm sorry."

"Just have faith, yeah?" Temple said. "The two people in there trying to save him are scary-smart, not to mention scary-determined. They're not going to let him get away with this stunt. Not without a fight."

Draven entered in time to hear the last part. He flopped down in an empty chair.

"How many people are ahead of me when it comes to thrashing him?" he asked, sounding tired.

"Five, I think," Skye said. "You might be able to take Ash's place, though. He doesn't look like he's really up to it at the moment."

"Line forms on the left," Temple repeated helpfully.

If anything, the mention of Ash made Draven's expression turn even sourer. "Fuckin' idiot," he said, and it wasn't immediately clear which one of his friends was the target of the insult.

"Yeah," Skye agreed darkly.

"I should've said something last night," Draven continued. "I knew Pax was acting strange. He's never once asked me for a single godsdamned thing. Like, *ever*. And then he suddenly wants me to pull a double shift and take his watch for him? Pats me on the back and tells me goodbye on his way out? Not even goodnight. *Goodbye*. *I'm* the idiot."

"It's not your fault," Temple said. "He was acting weird even before that, and none of us called him on it."

Skye nodded. "That part after the test with the virus, where he was talking about his 'appreciation for our willingness to assist him in this matter'?"

Temple nodded. "And about how he 'valued our association.' Yeah, that was weird. We all should have paid more attention, but no one would have guessed he'd pull something this... this..."

"Stupid?" Draven asked.

"Exactly," Temple said on a sigh.

"He'll be fine," Skye insisted stubbornly. "And then we'll all take turns kicking his ass and convince him not to do shit like this again."

"Agreed," Temple said.

"Agreed," Draven echoed.

"But what if he's not fine?" Nahleene asked.

"*He'll be fine*," Skye repeated, with more heat this time.

The next few cycles passed with tortuous slowness, the others coming and going so that Nahleene was never left alone. Finally, Ryder came in, looking exhausted and stony-faced. Nahleene shot to her feet. Ryder must have paged the others from the medbay, because they hurried into the canteen moments after her. Only Ash was absent.

"Well?" Nahleene demanded.

"He's physically stable," Ryder said. "We were able to bodge together a basic program to oversee his existing nanobot population. I'm not going to be able to simply filter them out of his bloodstream or program them all to deactivate and break themselves down. His body has become too reliant on them over the years. His native immune system is nonexistent at this point, and several of his major organs have become essentially symbiotic with them."

"What about his mental state?" Nahleene asked desperately. "You said *physically* stable."

"Like Ash told us before, half of Pax's mind is gone. He reinstalled the blueprint he had stored on an external hard drive, but all the data—all the actual knowledge Pax amassed and stored in the technologically enhanced portion of his brain has been wiped. He's currently scoring a four on the Grenvell coma scale. That's one point higher than the minimum possible score, and firmly in the range with the worst prognosis for recovery. There's no way of knowing how the sudden loss of his cyber brain will affect what's left in the long term."

Nahleene felt her expression harden. "Yes, there is. *I* know, because I've been in his mind—a full connection without shields on either side. I can't pick up a damned thing from his tech. It's physically impossible for me to do so. But the mind I touched—his *organic* mind—made up one pretty amazing man. He doesn't need the tech. But he needs *me*. You have to let me link with him... you have to let me try to pull him back."

She was vaguely aware that several of the others were exchanging surprised looks, though at least they were doing so silently. Apparently the details of her recovery a few days ago—and its embarrassing aftermath—hadn't become grist for the gossip mill.

Ryder gave her a narrow look, and she returned it.

"I'll allow it as long as you fully understand the risk it poses to your safety," the medic said after a lengthy pause. "But not right now. I want you fully rested before you attempt anything like that. And, even more importantly, I want to give Pax's bots more time to repair the organ damage that occurred during the hours his systems were degraded."

Nahleene clenched her jaw, aware that the prospect of her sleeping right now was about as likely as the prospect of the Vitharan government welcoming her back with open arms. But she could understand the need for Pax's body to heal before undergoing another potentially stressful undertaking.

"Fine," she said. "But you'll have to give me a mild sedative or there's no way I'll be getting any rest. And I'm sleeping in the medbay in case he takes a turn for the worse and I need to try emergency measures."

"I'll bring in a third cot," Ryder said, her voice tired.

"A *third* cot?" Draven asked sharply.

"I hit Ash with a sedative to get him off his feet once it was apparent that the cyborg upload was working properly," she said. "He'll probably be pissed at me when he wakes up a dozen cycles or so from now."

"Get the cot," Nahleene said. "And wake me up as soon as Pax is strong enough for me to attempt a link."

Nahleene awoke to a hand on her shoulder and a feeling of fuzzy-mouthed grogginess. She blinked until Ryder's grim and exhaustion-lined face came into focus. The events of last night crowded into her awareness, clamoring for immediate attention.

"Pax… how is he?" she asked, her tongue feeling thick and slow.

"Physically improved, mentally the same," Ryder said. "Get cleaned up, eat and drink something, then if you still want to try this, come back when you're ready."

"Of course I still want to try it," Nahleene said. "This is his best chance. Maybe his *only* chance."

Ryder met her gaze squarely. "You should know that I'm breaking a dozen different rules of medical ethics by doing this," she said. "You're already aware that I've been stripped of my license for ethics violations, of course, so it's not as though I'm covering virgin ground. But even so, the plain truth is that this could be dangerous for you, and I'm letting you do it anyway because I care for Pax and would grasp at any chance to help him—even a dangerous chance."

Nahleene stared at her. "Is this supposed to change my mind or something?"

Ryder sighed. "No. No, it's not. I already told you, I'll risk your safety for the chance of getting him back. I'm just easing my guilty conscience in advance... making sure I can tell myself afterwards that you knew the risks going in, in case something happens to you."

"That's fair enough," Nahleene told her. "In fact, if it helps, you should know that I would have snuck in at the first opportunity and tried it behind your back if you hadn't allowed it."

"I do know that," Ryder told her. "It's part of the reason I was able to talk myself into letting you try it under medical observation. At least it's a bit safer that way."

"Whatever you need to tell yourself," Nahleene said, aware that if she managed to lose herself inside a comatose mind, medical observation wouldn't make much difference to the grim outcome. "I'll be back shortly."

She swung to her feet, wavering a bit under the remnants of the sedative, and gave Pax's unmoving form a long look before heading out to get some food and use the lav. When she returned less than half a cycle later, he looked exactly the same as he had when she'd left. Ryder had taken him off life support at some point, but he was still far too pale and his features looked sunken, like he'd aged decades in the hours since he'd left her alone in her quarters the previous evening.

"Where's everyone else?" she asked absently. "It's quiet out there."

"I sent Ash back to his quarters, and the others are attempting to find out if the virus infected the cyborgs on the orbital platform, or if this entire stunt was for nothing," Ryder said.

"Have you slept?" Nahleene asked, taking in the lines of fatigue on Ryder's face and the dark circles under her eyes.

"Don't make me laugh," said the medic. "I'll sleep either when he wakes up and is stable, or after I confirm brain death. Now, are you still set on doing this?"

"What do you think?" Nahleene shot back. "One thing first, though. You want me to do this under medical observation. Fine. But if you *observe* me in distress and try to forcibly separate my mind from his, you're more likely to kill me than help me. Just so you know."

"I won't separate you," said Ryder. "Tell me what you need so we can get started."

Nahleene looked around. "Help me move this cot right up next to his. If I'm lying down, I won't be in a position to *fall* down when my mind gets too disconnected from my body. Also, turn the lights down to twenty-five percent or so. The glare is distracting."

Ryder helped her get things set up to her satisfaction, then dragged a chair over to the readout screen that would show results of the continuous medical scans she'd no doubt be performing. Nahleene arranged herself on the second cot, lying on her side facing Pax. From this position, the implants on the left side of his face were hidden from view, making him look like a perfectly normal Vithii male—albeit an incredibly strong and well-muscled one.

"I might speak words or phrases aloud," Nahleene warned. "They could be random and nonsensical, or not. If I do speak, it's not a cry for help. None of it's directed toward you. Let me do this, and don't try to interfere."

"I won't, unless it's to perform resuscitation on one or both of you," Ryder said grimly. "Just... try to bring him back to us."

"That's the plan," Nahleene told her, and reached out one hand to splay over the side of Pax's face.

EIGHTEEN

At first, mental contact with Pax's unconscious mind was much as it had been when she'd found him collapsed in the observation dome—a blank landscape with soft, staticky whispers barely audible in the background. Nahleene let herself float, taking time to get her bearings. She thought back to what it had felt like to meld with his mind after she'd woken from surgery, her telepathic senses scrambled.

On that occasion, she'd kept herself tethered to her own body—at least to start with. She'd told Pax to remove her hand from his face if he needed her to break the contact. If that had happened, it would have been painful, but her mind would have automatically snapped back within the bounds of her physical form. Now, though, she needed to stretch further. She needed to give herself complete freedom to reach the depths of his being, where whatever remained of him was hidden.

She took a deep breath, and cut the tether with her physical form.

Her heart would continue to beat; her lungs, to draw breath... at least for a while. But her mind was connected only to Pax, now. If she didn't succeed in dragging him back from whatever abyss he'd fallen into... if she couldn't retrace her psychic steps and return to herself, her body would eventually die, a mindless husk no different from his.

With steely determination, Nahleene flung herself toward the distant whisper of mental white noise. There was no true direction within a psychic communion such as this, but her awareness classified the way she was going as *down*. What remained of Pax was buried deep, his organic mind attempting to escape the shock of the virus attack by seeking oblivion.

Normally, the mind of an unconscious or comatose person whose psyche was still salvageable would be humming with confused memories and thoughts. The eerie quiet of her surroundings made Nahleene want to panic—made her fear there was nothing left of Pax—but she remembered how it had felt to touch his mind when he was whole. Even then, she could only access his experience of the here-and-now, with none of the usual confusion of background thoughts.

At the moment, the only thing he was experiencing was unconsciousness, so her inability to feel the random mental jetsam and flotsam didn't mean he was necessarily gone. She just needed him to experience something she could latch onto.

Pax! she cried mentally, channeling all of her telepathic power into the silent shout.

There was no response, and she chastised herself. He was psi-null, damn it. He couldn't hear her thoughts; he could only feel her emotions. She needed to reach him another way. She thought of the feelings that had been growing inside her over the past few days... the giddy, unexpected—and frankly rather terrifying—sense that she was falling for him, and falling hard. She thrust that feeling into the dark void around her, aware that it was weakened and distorted by her fears that he saw her as nothing more than a foolish meatbag, ruled by emotions that he could never return and would never want to.

Again, nothing stirred in the darkness.

Changing tack, she marshaled all of her fear and grief at the idea of losing him. She thought of what his loss would do to her. She thought of what it would do to his friends, remembering Ash's chalky face when he'd arrived to find that Pax had used the virus on himself, and Ryder's stony determination to try anything possible to save him.

Still, there was no change in the emptiness surrounding her, no increase in the volume of the distant whispering.

Bracing herself, Nahleene prepared to dive even deeper into the recesses of his mind. An instant later, she realized that she'd lost track of which direction was *deeper*, and which direction led back toward her body. She twisted in place, trying to orient herself based on the distant white noise, but it now seemed to be coming from all directions equally.

Panic jolted her, primal and raw. She'd taken too long… ventured too far. She was trapped. She couldn't even pick a direction at random—direction here was an illusion. A construct of her own consciousness. Mental travel was only meaningful if the person traveling knew where they were going, and… she didn't, anymore. She was in an endless void, and she'd lost her hold on the invisible piece of string leading back to herself.

Nahleene had failed, and now she wouldn't be able to save either of them. Terror gripped her—the terrible sinking feeling of realizing that no one would be coming to help her, and this utter, dark aloneness was all she would know until her eventual death. Gods... how long would it take? Would she be stuck in this state of mortal fear for hours? Days? Weeks?

Eternity?

Already, she could feel bits of herself spinning off like fractals into the nothingness—the first hint of approaching madness and the dissolution of self. Maybe this was the same thing Pax had felt as the virus ate away at his cybernetic brain?

The awareness of being unmade.

I'm sorry, I'm sorry, I'm sorry, I'm so, so sorry, she chanted, trying to stop the whirling pieces of herself from flying away into the darkness.

The fear was so all-consuming that she didn't notice the distant, confused whispers growing into something else until they were nearly upon her—a wall of invisible wind. The force hit her from all sides at once, driving her swirling pieces back together into some kind of a coherent whole. Suddenly, the background noise was no longer background noise, but a single, focused thought.

Nahleene... danger... help her.

Everything whipped sharply back into place like an elastic band snapping, and Nahleene was no longer alone in a void—she was entwined with Pax inside Pax's mind, and he was hurtling them *up*, toward what she now recognized as the direction of consciousness. She clung to him and added her mental power to his, moving them even faster. At the same time, she let the emotions of utter relief and yes, damn it, *love*, flood through her and into his essence.

He hadn't been able to respond on his own behalf, but as soon as *she* was in danger, he'd rushed to the rescue without thought for his own weakness or terrible mental injury. He *was* weak, though. As they rose from the depths of his unconscious state, she could feel his mental strength flagging. She took over, winging them toward consciousness, keeping a tight hold on his mind while utilizing her mental shields to ensure that they didn't fall into the same kind of uncontrolled emotional feedback loop they'd experienced the last time she'd melded them together so closely.

Awareness of Pax's corporeal body and surroundings returned, followed closely by her awareness of the connection between them, leading back to her own body. She hovered for a moment, making certain his grip on consciousness would hold without her mental strength bolstering his. When she was confident that it would, she used the last of her endurance to flow through the connection and settle back inside the confines of her physical form. She opened her eyes with a gasp, as though surfacing from underwater. Pax echoed her, their lungs sucking in the station's dry, recycled air in perfect tandem.

Pax blinked rapidly, trying to pull his surroundings into focus. His body felt... wrong—heavy and weak in a way that had not afflicted him since the time before his cyber-conversion. His mind reached for the data regarding how many years, months, and days it had been since he'd last felt this way, only to find a blank gap where the information should be. He was missing vast swathes of data, leaving only emptiness where digital memory ought to be housed.

Older memories insisted that panic should be the expected reaction to this discovery, but he couldn't feel panic. He couldn't feel *anything* except a wash of sweet relief. But that didn't make sense. He'd become a cyborg. He remembered that part. His emotional centers had been removed. How was he able to feel relief?

The answer came a moment later when he became aware of the warmth of fingertips splayed over the side of his face. *Nahleene*. Nahleene was touching him. She had been inside his mind. Something had happened, putting her in danger. He'd tried to help, and now she was relieved because the danger was past. It was *Nahleene's* relief he was feeling.

Her fingers left his face, and the sense of relief faded, leaving cold nothing behind, terrible in its yawning hollowness. He fumbled for her hand, his muscles not cooperating.

"Don't—" he rasped, not recognizing his own voice.

"*Pax.*"

That was a different voice. Female, but not Nahleene. A hand clasped his shoulder, but no wash of borrowed emotion followed. He rolled his head to the side. Red hair. A humming medical scanner hovering over his face.

"Ryder," he managed in a croak.

The hand squeezed his shoulder almost painfully before letting go. "Oh, thank the *gods*." An audible swallow as Ryder's throat bobbed up and down, once. "Pax—do you know where you are? What's the last thing you remember?"

He thought back, trying to maneuver around the places inside him that no longer existed. What did he remember?

"Stars," he said. "And... a face?"

"You were in the observation dome. Nahleene found you," Ryder said.

He cast his mind back further, thoughts seeming to take twice as long to come to him as they should.

He'd gone to the observation dome...

Because he'd needed to be alone so that...

So that... he could...

Oh. Right.

"The virus," he said. "Did it work?"

Ryder sucked in a sharp breath, her face growing thunderous for a moment before she hid the reaction behind an emotionless mask. But he was distracted from her expression by someone else's fingers clamping around his bicep, the nails digging in like claws. Rage slammed into him, taking his breath away and driving out the hollow feeling.

"*Did... it... work?*" Nahleene echoed, biting off each word viciously. "Are you fucking *joking*? That's it—I'm jumping the ass-kicking queue, right here and now. The others will just have to wait."

"You're not thrashing him right now, Veila'ana," Ryder said in a hard tone. "For one thing, you're about two seconds from keeling over. Let go of him."

"*No*," Pax gasped, and two angry sets of eyes settled on him.

"'No' to what?" Ryder asked.

"Don't... let go of me," he implored, catching and holding Nahleene's pale gaze. "It's too empty without your mind touching mine."

Nahleene's expression of anger collapsed into something much more painful to watch. He realized that she was sitting on a cot pushed flush against the one he was on, her legs curled beneath her. She wavered for a moment, her eyes going shiny with wetness, before she half-collapsed across his body, clutching him.

"Godsdamnit, Pax," she said into the space beneath his collarbone. "Gods*damn*it."

Ryder cleared her throat. "We're not having the virus conversation yet, all right? I don't know if it worked or not, Pax. The others are trying to find that out, which is a bit of a challenge since it's a secret program and we're stuck way the fuck out here in the badlands. For now, though, you both need to rest. Nahleene, can you tell if he's stable?"

"Yes," Nahleene said. "As long as I'm touching him, I'll know if he starts to slip and I can stop it."

"All right." Ryder looked at Pax again, frustrated. "Pax, I—" She cut herself off. "Never mind."

"I regret that my actions caused you and the others pain," he said quietly.

"Is that right? Well, you obviously didn't regret it *enough*," she said, and left the room.

Silence fell. Pax let the roiling emotions reaching him through the telepathic bond distract him from the overwhelming wrongness of everything around him and within him.

"I didn't expect to survive," he mused.

"I know," Nahleene said, not moving or loosening her grip on him. "But you did survive, and now you'll have to deal with the consequences of that."

NINETEEN

Somewhat unexpectedly, Pax slept. Actually *slept*, in the way that organics sleep, with the darkness and the time loss and the brush of Nahleene's borrowed dreams flickering through his mind. When he woke up, she was still in his arms, and Ash was seated in a chair nearby, watching him.

"I didn't design that bloody virus just so you could use it on yourself," Ash said without preamble, and there was no mistaking the cold anger in his tone.

"I know you didn't," Pax said.

Nahleene slept on, curled against his side, clearly still exhausted. For his part, Ash looked somewhat improved compared to the last time Pax had seen him.

"Don't ask me to do things for you and then throw them back in my face like this," Ash continued. "I refuse to be the reason any of you die."

"I'm not dead," Pax noted reasonably.

"Not my point," Ash bit out.

"But… I'm not fully functional, either," Pax admitted. "What did this do to me? So much is gone."

"*No shit.* What did you *expect*?" Ash asked, giving no quarter. He took a deep breath, as though trying to center himself. "Your decade-plus of accumulated cyber-data is gone. As far as I can determine, your brain stored facts and figures in the database, while more personal memories went in the organic brain. You clearly remember me, Ryder, and the ambassador, even though we never met you until after you were converted. I assume you remember the others, as well?"

"Yes," he said, thinking of Hunter, Kade, Draven, Skye, and Temple.

"But I expect you'll draw a blank if I ask you for the specs on Kade's fighter."

Pax tried to call up the engine thrust ratios... the weapons specifications... the year of manufacture. Nothing. "You would be correct. It is... disconcerting."

"Witness my deep and abounding sympathy," Ash said, expressionless. After a moment, he sighed. "You can upload any data that's publicly available to start filling in the gaps on technical knowledge and the like—though organizing it is going to be a serious bitch. Obviously, that won't help with personal information—dates and trivia and so forth. But again, you had to know this would happen, and you decided to *fucking do it anyway*."

Actually, Pax hadn't known this would happen. He thought he'd be dead, or a vegetable, but he suspected saying so right now would be impolitic. So, he changed the subject instead.

"Is there any news about the reanimated cyborgs?" he asked.

"Not yet," Ash said. "Kade is trying to get information through some of his contacts in the Capital. I need to get back there post-haste, myself. I can't take the courier ship and leave the rest of you stuck here with only a couple of two-seat fighters for transport, so he's going to run me back to Ilarius and drop me off before returning. Hopefully he'll be able to get a firm answer from his hired snoops while he's there."

Pax nodded. "Assuming they haven't somehow blocked my distress beacon from D-8's systems, I see no reason why it won't have worked. The virus seems... highly effective."

"Fuck you, Pax," Ash said, low and vehement.

Next to him, Nahleene blinked awake and stretched, looking around. "Oh," she said. "Hello. Are we doing the ass-kicking now?"

Nahleene rolled upright. She kept a hand on Pax's bare arm, remembering his rather heart-wrenching plea earlier not to let go of him. She could barely imagine what the experience of losing his cybernetic technology felt like from his perspective, and while they would eventually have to deal with the fallout, if she could make things easier for him right now by staying in mental contact with him, she would do so—no questions asked.

But that didn't mean she was ready to let him off the hook, and from what she'd just heard, neither was Ash.

"No," Ash said, "no arse kicking yet. And I'm leaving now, anyway, so give my spot to someone deserving. I was second in line after Ryder."

The door opened again, and Kade entered, eyeing Pax critically. "You're awake? Good. Never do something that stupid again. What the fuck kind of plan was that anyway?" He shook his head. "Ash, are you done haranguing him? Ready to go?"

"Yes, I'm ready. Pax, I'm quite cross with you at the moment, but seeing as the important parts of you seem to have survived, I expect I'll get over it. I'll... be in touch." Ash met Nahleene's eyes. "Ambassador—"

She cut him off. "Thank you for helping save his life," she said, and reached out her hand.

"I could say the same. In fact, I believe that makes two of my friends you've saved now," he replied, clasping her extended hand in a cool, firm grip. "It was a pleasure to meet you in person. Look after him, will you?"

A tangle of thoughts brushed across her awareness, a bit muddled since she was also in contact with Pax.

Hate lying to them don't want to do this what if it's the last time I ever see them I'm not even saying goodbye properly—

She blinked, and Ash released her hand, his face still cool and composed.

"What—" she began, but he was already turning away, heading for the door.

"Take care, both of you," he said over his shoulder. "Hopefully Kade will have some good news when he gets back."

"Be safe, Ash. Kade," Pax said, and Nahleene saw Ash's shoulders tense.

"I'll return sometime late tomorrow," Kade said. "With luck, your asinine plan will have born fruit. When I find out, I'll let you know."

The door slid shut behind them. Nahleene frowned.

"Something has disturbed you," Pax said. "I can... feel... concern?"

She looked down at him. "Ash is upset. He's... frightened, for lack of a better term."

Pax's features settled into hard lines. "Ash is undertaking a dangerous mission. I believe... some of the details must have been with my lost data, but... it's the reason he was injured when he arrived. It's affecting him psychologically as well as physically, but he considers the potential reward worth the risk to himself."

Something clicked into place in her mind. "Is the mission to do with the Terra Novan ambassador?" she asked.

Pax paused as though looking inward. "I'm sorry. I no longer have the answer to that question. Hunter will know. Whatever the case, Ash has managed to stay alive so far, if not precisely unharmed. We must have faith in his ability to follow his chosen course."

Her mouth twisted unhappily, but she knew she'd be a terrible hypocrite if she claimed not to believe that some things were worth personal risk— even the risk of death. She hoped Ash was successful in his mission, and not at too great a cost.

Over the next few cycles, the others trailed in singly or in pairs. Nahleene eventually had to break contact with Pax, for the simple reason that she needed to use the lav. He did not seem as obviously distressed as he had right after he'd awoken, so she contented herself with brushing her hand across his every so often between rounds of visitors.

To her not-very-great surprise, the ass kicking never truly materialized, though there was certainly a fair amount of heartfelt verbal abuse. Skye and

Draven each hugged Pax after they finished expressing how incredibly pissed off they were with him, and Hunter cupped a hand around the nape of his neck in an intimate fraternal gesture.

Eventually, Nahleene found herself sitting around the medbay with Pax, Temple, and Ryder, the others having left for various duties. Ryder had run Pax through a basic physical assessment, and reported no obvious deficits in his balance or reflexes.

"My heads-up display is nonfunctional," Pax complained during the vision test, peering at the eye chart curiously.

"Maybe you can reinstall something similar," Ryder said. "You and Kade should take a look at the hard drive Ash used to rebuild your basic systems. See what's there and what's not."

"Agreed," Pax said absently, still looking around the medical bay as though it was completely unfamiliar. Perhaps it was, without whatever ancillary data he was used to calling up at will.

"There's going to be a definite adjustment period," Ryder replied, grim.

Pax drew his attention fully back to her. "Indeed. I... find myself somewhat overwhelmed by the prospect. Also, unsure of my mental state with so much of myself irretrievably gone."

Temple shifted in his chair. "Right. This sounds like doctor-patient confidentiality territory to me. I think I'll leave you to it."

"I'm not a doctor, Temple," Ryder said in a tired voice.

Temple smiled. "Whatever you say, Red." He placed a human-style kiss on her forehead. "You've still been keeping doctor's hours these past couple of days, so come back to our quarters soon and get some damned sleep." Nahleene looked away politely as Temple nipped Ryder's earlobe and added, "I'll be sure to make it worth your while," in a low murmur.

He straightened, giving her and Pax a quick, tired smile as he left the room, the door sliding shut behind him on rusty tracks. Ryder watched him go fondly before giving Pax her full attention.

"Would you like Nahleene to stay for this conversation?" she asked, and Nahleene realized with a small shock that she hadn't even considered following Temple's lead by offering to give him privacy.

"Yes," Pax said, his eyes coming to rest on her. "If you are willing. It does involve you rather intimately."

And what the hell was wrong with her that his last few words made a blush stain her cheeks copper? *Fucking prophets...*

"Of course I'll stay," she managed. "Like it or not, I've kind of become tangled up with your mental state."

The intensity of his regard made her feel as though he were trying to read something into her statement, beyond the general sense of '*this whole thing is a clusterfuck and I'm part of it*' that she'd intended to convey.

He merely nodded, though, before continuing. "I am uncertain how to continue as I am. I have become neither Vithii nor cyborg. Before I entered the program, I never mourned my lack of cyber-enhancement. After I was enhanced, I never mourned the lack of my former existence as a feeling, organic being. How could I, with my emotions gone? Now, however, I am missing both of those things, and the emptiness is palpable. It makes it difficult for me to... function."

Ryder leaned back in her chair, clearly choosing her words. "Pax. You've undergone what is essentially a massive traumatic brain injury. There's no avoiding the fact that your life has changed. That said, you have a distinct advantage over someone with an organic brain injury, in that the infrastructure is in place inside your databanks for the recovery of much of what you lost. True, some of your personal data can't be replaced, and there are many things that you probably won't realize you're missing until you need them and they're not there. But the void you described won't always be present. You'll fill it up with new data as time goes on."

"And the void of my lost emotions?" Pax asked. "The parts of me that were torn out to turn me into a weapon?"

Ryder tilted her head. "That's a much harder question."

"I disagree," Pax told her. "The answer is that they're gone."

A lump rose in Nahleene's throat.

"Yes," Ryder agreed, "they are. But the question I was referring to is what has changed that makes you more aware of the loss, and how that awareness can be ameliorated."

"It's because of me, isn't it?" Nahleene blurted.

Ryder looked at her curiously. "Without you, we wouldn't be having this conversation in the first place, since he'd be brain-dead."

"That's not what I mean, though," she said. "It's because I forced emotion on him—starting back on Ilarius, the night we met. Is that it, Pax?"

Pax opened his mouth to reply, but Ryder cut him off.

"Back up a minute. You *what*, now?" she asked. "Nahleene, Pax is physiologically incapable of experiencing emotion. That's just a biological fact."

"Your statement is inaccurate," Pax said. "I am physiologically incapable of *producing* emotion. I seem to be... more than capable of experiencing someone else's."

Ryder looked like someone had just smacked her in the face. "You can feel Nahleene's emotions when she's in contact with you? They affect you?"

"Yes," he said simply.

"That's..." Her mouth opened and closed a couple of times. "I have no idea how that's even possible." She was silent for a moment, thinking. "But, then, I have no idea how it's possible that you spontaneously regained your free will and threw off the yoke of your programming, either. So, what do I know, right?"

The lump in Nahleene's throat grew larger. "I never had any intention of hurting you like that, Pax."

Pax only blinked at her. "I do not hurt," he said. "Not unless you are hurting while you are in contact with me. I merely... *lack*."

Ryder blew out a breath. "Well, shit. I suppose, for what it's worth, there's no real reason, going forward, why the two of you would need to have telepathic contact again. It's possible that the effect will fade over time, Pax. Most things do, in my experience."

The lump became an ache and spread lower, into Nahleene's chest. Her future unspooled before her—leaving this outpost, contacting Vithara, perhaps fleeing to Maelfius or some other neutral planet to escape prosecution and imprisonment for espionage. Never seeing Pax or any of his friends again.

"I didn't mean for my actions to affect you like this," she said around that heavy ache, calling on her years of hiding her true self to make the words come out level. "Ryder's right. If we stay away from each other, maybe things will go back to how they were before."

A furrow formed between Pax's brows. "I do not want to stay away from you. Rather the opposite, in fact. I find that I never wish to let you go."

Surprise made the breath catch in Nahleene's chest.

"*Oh*-kay, then," Ryder said, pushing up from her chair. "Looks like Temple had it wrong. This isn't a *doctor-patient confidentiality* conversation. It's a *you-and-her* conversation. Pax, you seem physically stable, and I see no reason you can't get out of this med-bay as long as you don't push yourself too hard. Nahleene, I trust you to know what the hell's going on with your telepathic abilities better than I do—you've already proven that. Just... don't break him, all right? In the mean time, I'm going to bed. Call me if you need me. Otherwise, come back and see me tomorrow morning."

"All right," Nahleene said, still shell-shocked.

A moment later, Ryder was gone, leaving behind a silence heavy with tension and possibility.

TWENTY

Nahleene's reaction made Pax suspect that speaking so bluntly had been a mistake. He knew that he had even less to offer her now than he'd had before using the virus on himself. And he had already decided before then that he had nothing of substance to offer a lover.

The silence stretched, and he had no idea how to break it in a way that might prove productive. Finally, Nahleene took a deep breath and spoke.

"Come with me," she said. "I don't want to have this conversation in a medical bay."

He nodded and let her lead him outside, into the station corridor. With a shock, he realized that his mental map of the station was gone. He had no idea how to navigate it and could not have said where any of the rooms were, though he could picture several of their interiors in his mind.

Thankfully, that would be easily remedied by copying a map from the station computers, but it was still disquieting. He followed Nahleene through a maze of hallways until they fetched up in front of a door identical to all the others. It opened into the observation dome. The room carried two strong associations—holding Nahleene as she slept, and lying back on the couch as he slotted the micro-drive containing the virus into place.

"Before you ask," Nahleene said, "yes, being in this room does bring back very unpleasant memories of finding you comatose on that sofa and thinking you were dead. However, it also happens to be the most beautiful place in the station, and I don't care to have it permanently ruined. So we're going to talk right here, under the stars."

The door closed behind them. She engaged the privacy lock before turning back to look deeply into his eyes in the dim light.

"Tell me something truthfully," she said, and held out her right wrist, palm up. The stars barely illuminated a dark mark, which was slowly fading as the bruise healed. "Why did you give me this before you went off to kill yourself with the virus?"

"I did not kill myself," he said after a faint pause, not sure why he felt the need to drive the point home when it was already obvious. "I'm right here."

"You *thought* it would kill you," she said. "Don't try to claim that you didn't."

That was difficult to counter, since it was true. Still, he needed her to understand. "My intention in using the virus was not to end my life. My intention was to end the cyborg program."

"I get that," Nahleene said. "You think I don't, but you're wrong. I do. Now, answer the question. Why did you give me a Vitharan love mark before marching off to risk your life in secret?"

The answer required no thought. "Because I wished you to remember me, and to know how much I valued the short time we had together," he said.

She lifted her chin. "Would you have given me that mark if there was no virus? If you'd had no reason to think you wouldn't see me again soon?"

He considered for a moment. "No."

"Why not?" she asked.

"Because it would have implied that I wished you to continue as my lover," he told her, "and I had already determined that your attaching yourself to me in such a way would not be beneficial for you."

Her eyes burned holes in him. "And you didn't think that maybe it would be better to give me a say in that decision?"

He stared right back at her, brow furrowing. "I was concerned that you might feel the need to act out of obligation for some perceived debt. You seemed very certain that you owed me something after melding with my mind when you were recovering from the removal of the telepathic blocking implant."

Now, her expression grew incredulous. "And you thought I might continue as your lover because I felt bad about joining minds with you and then fucking you?"

He opened his mouth, and closed it again. Somehow when she phrased it that way, his unassailable logic suddenly seemed a bit more... *assailable*.

"I had very little to offer you, even then," he tried instead. "Though I have even less to offer you now."

"And I repeat— maybe it would be better to give me a say in that decision?" she said dryly.

He shook his head—not really a negation of her words, but more a gesture of confusion over them. "Why would you possibly want to tie yourself to someone who could never feel emotion for you? Someone who could never... *love* you in the way you deserve to be loved?"

She raised a slow eyebrow at him. "So, you're saying that you conflate *feeling* love with *understanding* love," she said. "Interesting."

It took a moment for him to make the connection, but apparently that particular conversation was lodged firmly in the organic part of his brain. The context came flooding back, followed closely by the sense of several assumptions reshuffling themselves within his mind.

"You... believe that being with someone who only possessed an understanding of love rather than the feeling of love would be... sufficient for you?" he asked carefully, not wishing to risk misunderstanding.

Nahleene's hand came up to cup his cheek—not the purposeful placement she'd used to initiate close telepathic contact in the past, but rather in a gesture of tenderness. However, that didn't stop a new emotion from flooding him—one he identified as cautious hope.

"Pax," she said, "I've watched you act against near-impossible odds to ensure that the minds of your deceased batch siblings weren't misused. I've watched you care for your friends' emotional needs. I've seen you risk your life and your mental wellbeing for me—a relative stranger. I know damned well that you only used that virus on yourself so no one else would be endangered during a direct assault on the cyborg program. Don't even talk to me about understanding love."

Her hand was still on his face, and the growing surge of her emotions against him contained a wild tangle of relief, worry, guilt, hope, and something huge and deep and terrifying that he'd not felt since he was a child, while surrounded by his family's steadfast support.

Something that he felt fairly certain was love.

Woven all through it was her fervent desire to be closer—for Pax to take her in his arms and crush her body against his. So that was what he did. And it felt...

It felt better than anything else he could ever remember experiencing in his life, even before he'd been changed.

"Is this a 'yes, I'm willing to try'?" Nahleene whispered against his chest, her free arm squeezing him just as hard as he was squeezing her.

"Yes, Nahleene. I am willing to try," he said, his voice emerging oddly unsteady.

"Good," she said breathlessly. "Now take me to bed, godsdamnit."

He looked around the quiet, peaceful space with a myriad of stars winking overhead—beautiful to him now that he could see them once more through the lens of her emotions.

"No," he said. "Not to bed. I'd much rather take you right here."

Nahleene clung to the strong body holding her close, glad now that she'd thought to palm the privacy lock after they came in. Pax's words kindled a slow burn of heat in her belly, and with her body pressed against his, she felt her desire awaken his through the light telepathic bond initiated by her touch.

One of his large hands trailed down her back to cup her buttock, pulling her hips flush against his hardening length. This time, she was in a far better position to fully appreciate everything that was happening, and she intended to make the most of it.

"Clothes," she ordered, wanting access *right now* to all those hard planes and rippling muscles she'd gotten to enjoy so briefly in the cramped station shower. The only downside was that to get their clothing off, she'd have to break contact with him. At least the jumpsuit she'd borrowed from Ryder opened with a simple zipper down the front, and there was nothing terribly complicated about his form-fitting black shirt and trousers.

He let her pull the shirt over his head, her fingers trailing along his sides as she lifted it off. Then he was pulling the zipper on her jumpsuit down, revealing the fact that she'd drawn the line at asking to borrow someone else's underwear even though hers was a complete tragedy after several stressful days. She'd decided it was easier to go without, and now the feeling of crisp polysynth sliding down her bare skin made her feel wanton.

The feeling obviously transmitted itself to Pax, because he made a low sound in the back of his throat that did nothing to quell the fire of need growing inside her. She attacked the closure of his trousers while attempting to simultaneously shimmy free of the half-discarded flightsuit. Pax toed off his heavy boots and let her pull his trousers and briefs off together.

At which point, she ended up crouched at eye level with his twitching cock, both of them finally, gloriously naked. Prophets, he was fucking huge. Of course, the rest of him was fucking huge as well, so it's not like this should have come as a complete shock. But somehow, she'd failed to truly appreciate it before. Now, it made her sex pulse, begging to be filled and stretched, at the same time her mouth watered.

And, well, she was down here anyway, so...

She grasped him around the base, closing her hand around the part of him that would swell inside her, locking them together. He hissed out a breath between his teeth, the sound becoming a moan when she licked his twitching, seeking tip and closed her lips over it.

"Nahleene," he gasped, his hand tangling through her short spikes of hair

She got the sense it was more to steady himself against the unexpected sensation than to guide her movements. Vitharans weren't big on fellatio, as a rule—the men preferring to reach orgasm with their knots inside a nice warm, tight passage. Maelfians were all about oral sex, though, and Nahleene truly enjoyed the feeling of power that came from sucking a man.

She wouldn't bring Pax to orgasm this way—that wasn't what either of them wanted—but since she got off on sucking him, and his experience of what they were doing was closely dependent on hers, she'd damned well tease him a bit first.

Based on the way his hand tightened in her hair and his muscles trembled with the effort to stay still, it was working. The first drops of slick pulsed from his tip and she tongued him clean, savoring the salty-metallic taste.

"*Nahleene*," he rasped again, the trembling in his muscles growing more pronounced.

This time, she had pity on him, pulling away just in time for a fresh dribble of slick to appear in the slit at the end of his cock. She cupped him, letting some of it drip into her palm before fisting him with slow strokes to spread the natural lubricant over his length.

"Enough," he almost growled, his hand closing around her wrist and pulling her grip away from him. "No more teasing. I want to feel what makes you lose control beneath me. I want to feel you come, and feel your mind go soft and quiet inside mine while I knot you. Let me feel those things."

There was no question he felt the throb of lust that his words inspired, because an instant later, Nahleene was sprawled on the threadbare couch, her legs spread wide. She had a brief, unwanted flash of finding Pax laid out here like a corpse, but it was lost the moment he knelt and dragged her right leg over his shoulder. With no further warning, he bit the soft flesh of her inner thigh, just above her knee.

She arched, crying out, her hand scrabbling for a grip on... something. Anything. Her fingers found his arm and clung to it as he moved a few centimeters higher and bit down again. And again. Each time driving her a little crazier, making her cries a little louder. He worked his way up her inner thigh, bypassing her sex completely to suck marks onto her stomach and breasts.

"Thought you said no... *teasing*," she managed around a gasp.

"I said I wanted to feel what makes you lose control beneath me," he murmured against her breast, right before he bit down sharply on the point of her nipple. She keened and nearly arched off the damned sofa before he finally let the hard nub slip free of his teeth. "This seems to be working fairly well," he added a bit unsteadily.

She fell back, trembling, and looked down to see a landscape of bruises and bite marks littering her body. "F-fuck," she stammered, feeling like she was hovering on a knife's edge.

Pax closed his eyes, bringing her hand up to rest against the side of his face. "Yes," he whispered. "I do like this feeling rather a lot."

He made her wait until the sense of being poised over an abyss eased a bit for both of them. When she no longer felt like his first stroke inside her would make her body explode, he pressed her down to lie lengthwise along the couch, her head propped on one soft armrest. He was poised over her, bracing his weight easily on one arm while he used the other to hook her knee over his elbow.

The position splayed her open beneath him like one of those Terran butterflies in a museum, pinned in place and completely at his mercy. Her sex pulsed with need, the slick tip of his cock exploring her folds as though eager to burrow inside.

"Please," she begged, trying to wriggle and only succeeding in burrowing deeper into the cushions of the comfortable old couch.

"Yes," he breathed, and plunged into her, sheathing himself.

His size, combined with the position he held her in, made it feel like he was splitting her in two in the most delicious way, her flesh aching and fluttering as her body stretched to accommodate him. She groaned, distantly aware that he was attacking her neck, leaving his mark there, too. His lips were only centimeters from the vestigial lump of her mating gland, which tingled with desire for his teeth.

She hadn't thought to tell him about the details of her genetic makeup—that he could bite her there without truly binding them. And oh, how she wanted him to bite her there. Still, this wasn't the time to try to have any kind of a serious conversation. Not with her need and growing excitement echoing back at her from his mind, melding with his own approaching release.

The next time they did this, he would flip her over and enter her roughly from behind, clamping his teeth around the juncture of her neck and shoulder as her orgasm crashed over her. The mental image was enough to tip her over the edge, ripples of excruciating pleasure careening up and down her spine as her body clamped down hard around the cock twitching and swelling inside her.

He followed her into release, pulsing into her depths, his teeth still fastened to the side of her throat. He was silent as he came, but she felt his whole body arch and shudder with the force of his orgasm.

Her mind was already going hazy as he gathered her to him and somehow rolled them both over, so he was the one lying on his back with her body draped over his. She moaned as she felt his knot swell inside her, tying them together. A profound feeling of relief and freedom as her worries fell away flowed through the mental bond between them.

"I love you," she whispered through the endorphins flooding her body and mind.

"I understand how you feel," he murmured against the mark he'd left on her neck, as the coital trance took them both.

Above them, the stars twinkled like fairy lights, painting everything silver and ethereal.

The following evening, Nahleene and Skye lounged in the makeshift fitness room, witnessing the closest thing they were likely to get to Pax's ass kicking. Which... wasn't very close, to be honest.

As Ryder's confidence grew that there were unlikely to be further major complications in Pax's recovery from the virus, she encouraged him to start exploring its impact on his physical abilities. Nahleene might or might not have blushed like a damned virgin as her thoughts immediately dove for the gutter, but she did at least manage to keep herself from saying something appalling like, 'Physically, he's looking pretty great from my perspective—the man's hung like a *greilo*-beast, thanks for asking.'

Because apparently Ryder was referring to *other* things, like hand-to-hand combat and target practice. Not, you know... *sex*. And that was all right. Fighting and weapons skills were important, too—especially given the circumstances surrounding them. Plus, she couldn't deny that watching Pax wrestle Draven, both of them naked from the waist up, had its own rewards.

"I wonder if I could get Hunter down here?" Skye mused, making Nahleene think her mind might be running along similar tracks. "Maybe if he and Draven tagged teamed Pax, they could take him down."

It was true that Draven looked like he could use a bit of help right now. Pax might've lost speed and accuracy with firearms since losing most of his enhanced targeting software, but it appeared that his hand-to-hand combat skills had been laid down long before the Regime technicians pumped him full of cybertech. With Pax's bots now once again bolstering his physical strength and endurance, Draven was struggling to hold his own.

It wasn't due to any lack of strength or skill on his part, either—the guy was built like a small mountain. What he lacked in height, he more than made up for in bulk, and he was quick with it, too.

He was also outclassed, and he obviously knew it.

"Should've... thumped you... while you were still in... the medbay," he grated out, pausing between words to pant for air. He twisted, sweaty skin glistening, trying to slide free of the hold Pax had on him.

"Then you would have needed to take on Ryder before you even got to me," Pax said. "That sounds like poor strategy."

"Smug... bastard..." Draven gasped, and managed to slip free of Pax's grip so he could put some distance between them. Draven feinted left and came in low, driving a shoulder into Pax's stomach and tangling a foot behind his as he took a step back to compensate. Pax went down, taking Draven with him, and Nahleene might have applauded Draven's momentary advantage if she wasn't pretty sure Pax was going easy on his opponent.

For a second or two, it looked like Draven might be in with a chance as the pair grappled for the upper hand. Then, in a move almost to fast to follow, Pax twisted his body and pinned Draven face down. Draven's left arm flashed out as he attempted to right himself, but Pax caught his wrist and wrapped a leg over his shoulder to hyperextend the joint in what Nahleene recognized from her self-defense training as a modified coil lock.

"Fuck," Draven said into the mat.

Pax let him go and rose smoothly, offering Draven a hand up when he flopped onto his back and wiped the sweat from his face. Draven took Pax's hand with good grace and shook out his shoulder once he was upright.

"Either you've lost a bit of your ruthlessness or you were holding back," Draven said, grabbing a towel from one of the wall racks. "I'm guessing it was the latter?"

"Yes, I was holding back," Pax agreed. "It appears that my unarmed combat skills, at least, were not noticeably affected by the loss of data."

He hadn't even broken a sweat, but Nahleene still mourned the loss of the view when he crossed to retrieve his black shirt from a nearby weight bench and shrugged into it.

Since the show was over, Skye got to her feet and stretched. "Don't worry, Pax. You're still more accurate with a blaster than ninety percent of us meatbags, and you can get back the other ten percent if you work at it, I bet."

Nahleene sauntered over to give him a congratulatory hug.

"I will speak with Kade when he returns about attempting to replace some of my targeting and sensor software," Pax said, wrapping an arm around her. The door opened as he was speaking.

"Is someone in here taking my name in vain?" Kade asked.

"Hey, welcome back," Draven said. "Everything go smooth for you in the Capital?"

"As much as it ever does," Kade allowed. "Pax, I have news."

All the attention in the room instantly centered on him. Nahleene let Pax go and gave the back of his hand a bolstering brush of her fingertips as they approached Kade expectantly. He didn't make them wait.

"My contact intercepted several communications about a catastrophic failure within the cyborg R&D program," he said. "The government is trying to downplay it—"

"No surprise there," Draven muttered.

"—but it appears they've abandoned the latest experimental program after more than three-quarters of the test subjects underwent a complete and unexplained cascade failure. The remaining subjects were *decommissioned*, as a precaution." The word was delivered with a harsh sneer, and Nahleene shivered.

"What about the other cyborgs?" she asked. "The ones like Pax?"

"There aren't any other cyborgs like Pax," Kade said. "But to answer your question, there's no indication that the living cyborgs were affected by the virus."

"If the distress beacons usually just communicate between batch siblings, that makes sense," Draven offered. "They probably wouldn't have connected the experimental cyborgs with the existing active force. Too risky."

"Agreed," Pax said.

"It sounds like you did it, Pax," Skye observed quietly.

"So it appears," Kade agreed. "Not sure it's the kind of thing that calls for congratulations, but I guess it's better than you having fried your systems for nothing. Anyway, I dropped Ash off safely, and Hunter wants to meet with everyone first thing in the morning to discuss our next steps. This place isn't really set up for long-term habitation—not without shipping in more supplies."

Nahleene took a breath. "I've been thinking," she said, and tangled her fingers with Pax's so he would be able to gauge her emotions as she spoke. "I've been spying for Maelfius, as I'm sure you already suspected. I've broken several espionage laws on Vithara, and if I go back there, it's likely I'll face criminal prosecution. But I've been hesitant to seek asylum on Maelfius, for fear of raising tensions between Maelfius and Ilarius."

Skye gave her a curious look. "Can't you just sneak back? If no one knows you're there, no one can be pissed about it."

Nahleene gave her a wry smile. "That's what I finally realized, yes. The Vitharans know I survived the shuttle attack, but that's all they know. There's nothing to say I wasn't killed later, and I didn't tell them where I was or who I was with."

She looked up at Pax, who was staring at her intently, a frown furrowing his strong brow.

"I won't go alone, though," she continued. "I want to talk to Hunter in the morning, but, Pax, I'd like you to come to Maelfius with me in secret. They're the only ones I haven't betrayed. The Maelfian intelligence community is likely to listen to what I have to say about the Regime—about how dangerous it's becoming. Will you come with me and help me make them understand?"

Pax looked down at her, his fingers squeezing hers where they hung entwined.

"Of course I will come," he said. "I would follow you anywhere you asked, Nahleene."

Her heart swelled, the uncertainty of the future settling into the security of knowing that whatever happened, she would no longer have to face it alone.

Kade was nodding slowly. "I think your instincts are right on this. It's past time for us to look outward for help. We can't fight this alone, and if the Premiere isn't stopped soon, it won't just be Ilarius thrown into chaos. It'll be the entire Seven Systems." He took a deep breath and let it out slowly. "We'll iron out details tomorrow. But if you can somehow sway the Maelfian government, and if Ash can stay alive long enough to get the Terra Novan ambassador on board with us, maybe this isn't as much of a lost cause as it first appears."

"*Hope*," Skye said softly. "Prophets. I'd almost forgotten what that feels like."

Nahleene looked around the small group before her gaze once again caught and held on Pax's. "Yeah," she said. "I know what you mean. Hope is definitely a concept I can get behind."

EPILOGUE

Ash knelt on the cold floor of the brothel's dungeon, naked, with his arms bound tightly behind him. His eyes did not stray from the small patch of gray plasticrete between his knees as the Vithii Adjunct to the Clandestine Operations Office circled him slowly, with measured, deliberate steps.

"So. You finally wish to take my collar, human?" The lash of the Adjunct's favorite whip whispered over Ash's shoulder—the barest of touches—as the rough voice continued, "Why now?"

The whip's butt rested under Ash's chin, lifting his head from its bowed position. He looked through his lashes at the hulking figure standing over him, his face as still as marble despite the slow trickles of blood running down his chest and stomach from where the lash had already flayed his skin open.

"There are dangerous people after me, *Fei'graal*. I don't know how much longer I can evade them. I fear for my life as a human in the Capital, and for my parents' lives. You are the only one who can protect me. My purchase price will be enough to get my family off-planet," Ash said in a low, compelling tone. He knelt, calm and motionless—feeling nothing. His mind locked safely away from his surroundings as he continued, "In return for my parents' safety, I give you everything I am.

My freedom. My body. My personhood. All yours now, until death."

"Good." The whip disappeared, and Ash lowered his gaze again. "I was about to look elsewhere for a *veelaht*, you realize. You have made yourself unavailable to me. Not just once, but on multiple occasions, and often for days at a time. Count yourself lucky that I am a patient man."

Ash knew better than to respond. Fingers lifted the long hair hanging down his back, sliding through the loose strands as they arranged it to lie over his right shoulder. The plain leather 'house' collar provided by the brothel tightened and loosened as large hands unbuckled it. A moment later, a stiff new band circled his throat. It was cool, not yet warmed by his body heat.

As it pulled snugly against his skin, ice-cold prickles like frozen needles skittered down the length of Ash's spine. He schooled himself not to react outwardly, while inwardly, he drew his mind further inside the muffling walls of dissociation that separated who he was from what he sometimes allowed others to do to his body. The collar settled into place, fastened a couple of holes too tight.

No doubt, purposely so.

"We are done tonight. Go clean yourself up and complete whatever paperwork is necessary to satisfy the owners of this place. I will transfer the credits once I receive the documentation," said the Adjunct. "Speak to no one else. My driver will arrive at oh-eight-hundred tomorrow morning to transport you to my property outside of the Capital. You will be safe there."

"Yes, *Fei'graal*," Ash agreed. "And the issue we discussed?"

The sharp sting of the whip's lash across the top of his left thigh was not completely unexpected, but he couldn't control the jerk of his muscles in response.

"Such things are no longer your concern, *veelaht*. It will be as I agreed earlier."

A hand tangled in Ash's hair again, rough this time. It dragged his head back, arching his neck until the pull on his scalp grew painful and the edges of the collar bit into his skin. Ash held his breath, not even trying to draw air past the tight restriction. A few moments later, the hand shoved sideways, sending him sprawling with his bound arms trapped beneath him. He lay unmoving, not attempting to rise.

"Never presume to question me again, cur," said the Adjunct. "Remember—after tonight, I am no longer bound by the rules of this establishment when it comes to my conduct toward my property. Do you understand?"

Bitterness rose in Ash's throat upon hearing the undertone of excitement lurking behind the Vithii's words, but not a trace of it colored his soft reply.

"Of course, *Fei'graal*. I assure you... from now on, I am completely at your disposal."

And very soon, you idiot, your household will be at mine, he added silently. *Including the one person on this shithole of a planet who just might hate you as much as I do.*

finis

The *Love and War* series continues with Book 4: *Anthelion*.

To discover more books by this author, visit
www.rasteffan.com

Made in the USA
Las Vegas, NV
16 March 2021